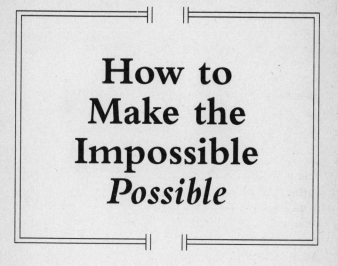

How to Make the Impossible *Possible*

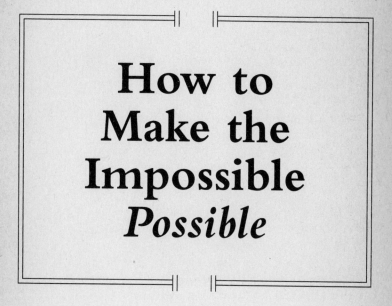

How to Make the Impossible *Possible*

DR. ROBERT ANTHONY

B

BERKLEY BOOKS, NEW YORK

HOW TO MAKE THE IMPOSSIBLE *POSSIBLE*

A Berkley Book / published by arrangement with
R.O.I. Associates, Inc.

PRINTING HISTORY
Berkley trade paperback edition / March 1996

ISBN: 0-425-14978-1

BERKLEY®
Berkley Books are published by The Berkley Publishing Group,
200 Madison Avenue, New York, New York 10016.
BERKLEY and the "B" design
are trademarks belonging to Berkley Publishing Corporation.

PRINTED IN THE UNITED STATES OF AMERICA

10 9 8 7 6 5 4 3 2 1

══╣ ACKNOWLEDGMENTS ╠══

I want to acknowledge the contribution that others have made in helping me to make the impossible possible. To Art and Lee Pitcher for their unconditional friendship and support over the past ten years. To Ramon and Patty Bonin for their friendship as well as their inspiration and dedication in promoting my work to others. To Lisa, my first true love, for showing me what was possible. To Cyndi for showing me what was impossible. To Jacqueline, whose love and dedication help to make all things possible. And, a very special thanks to Marti Jacobs, whose editorial assistance with this manuscript made this book possible.

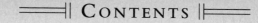

CONTENTS

CONTENTS

INTRODUCTION

Over the past fifteen years, I have written several books on success and positive living. I do not claim to have a corner on the truth, but over time, the principles outlined in my books have worked sucessfully for myself as well as my readers.

The interesting thing about life is that just when you think you have it figured out, a new lesson presents itself that you are totally unprepared for. Since I am a trained professional, it would seem that I would have an advantage over the average person when it comes to handling life's problems. That is not always true.

It's true that I have advanced skills in helping others, but when it comes to helping myself, another factor enters into the picture. That factor is human emotion. In other words, I am *personally* involved and less objective when it comes to handling my own problems or impossible situations.

Over the past few years, I have experienced some seemingly impossible situations. What surprised me was that the same principles I had been living by for years, which brought success in my personal and business life, seemed to be turning against me. In short, everything that could go wrong, did. This included my health, love relationship, and financial situation. It was almost as if something outside of me was out to get me. At first, I thought the situation was only temporary, and it would pass. Then, when it didn't, and got even worse, I started to lose faith in everything that I had believed.

For the most part, I try to live a positive lifestyle. I do my best to help others along the way by sharing my knowledge, my finances, and myself. Granted, I am human and often fall short of my true intentions, but I didn't think I deserved all my problems. In an effort to find answers, I asked myself, "Is this a test from God?" "Did I do this to myself?" Then I asked the ultimate stupid question, "Why me?" as though I were exempt because I am a good person. "Look at all those bad people who commit crimes, do drugs, and hurt others physically and emotionally. Why aren't all the bad things happening to them?"

What this book is about is my understanding of why things go wrong and what, if anything, we can do about them. Is positive thinking the answer? Is religion the answer? Is fighting back the answer? What do we do when there seems to be no answer? It took me almost three years to find out. During that time, I learned some important lessons about impossible situations. I also learned how to deal with these situations. Most of all, I learned that it wasn't personal.

Things happen for many reasons. What is most important is not the reason, but how we are going to handle what is in front of us. When I stopped taking the impossible situations personally and focused on possible opportunities, things began to change. My health improved, my finances jumped back, and an incredible love relationship fell into my lap without any effort on my part.

Rather than getting into the details of my impossible situations, I will emphasize what I *learned* from these situations. Again, I don't pretend to have all the answers, but I think you will find some interesting insights that will be helpful to you if you are currently facing what seems like an impossible situation.

I invite you to join me while I reinforce what I have learned. If it can help you in even a small way, this book was well worth the time and effort.

CHAPTER 1

Impossible Situations
When Things Look the Worst

SOMETHING WILL ALWAYS GO WRONG

Have you ever noticed that no matter what you do or how positive you are, something always seems to go wrong? It seems like there is one problem after another. We finally get one solved, and another one takes its place. You are having health problems, and when you finally are well, you are facing financial problems. Or you have financial problems and finally get them under control, and you are having a problem with your relationship. Sometimes everything seems to go wrong at the same time.

As much as we try, we just can't seem to find a way to live our lives without the constant barrage of problems. We read self-help books, listen to tapes, attend to our spiritual life, think positively, but life keeps presenting one problem after another for us to deal with. What's going on?

I might as well give you the bad news first. For as long as you are on the planet, your life will continue to be full of problems. Even those who just focus on the positive will continue to have problems. Optimists who assume "It won't happen to me" often learn, quite painfully, that it does happen to them. They overestimate their ability to accomplish and underestimate their resources and often end up in situations that cause serious problems.

The truth is that no matter what we do, how we think, or how we live our lives, there is no way we can avoid problems. A life without problems is not an option that is available to you, me, or anyone else. The reason for this is that *problems are normal and natural. They represent the difference between where you are and where you want to be.* Since there will always be a gap between where we are in any situation and where we want to be, our life is about *solving* problems. When you solve one problem, what's going to fill in that space? Another problem. I can guarantee you that every time you solve a problem, another one will come along.

Since we can't avoid problems, the key to happiness and sound mental health is the way we choose to *respond* to problems as opposed to trying to *avoid* them. How we perceive where we are and what we have and how we feel about it will determine what happens to us in the future. I am sure you have seen the bumper sticker that says, "Life's a bitch and then you die." I don't believe that, but whether it's true or not, one thing is for sure: What's important is not what happens to us but how we respond to what happens to us.

It is impossible to escape the fact that something will always go wrong. This is part of the ebb and flow of life. It is not so much that something is going wrong but our interpretation or view of what is happening. Anything that seems to go wrong is something that usually doesn't fit our cause-and-effect view of order. To assume that something has gone wrong is to assume that something is happening to us, either as an individual or collectively.

For the majority of people, life is often a desperate, frustrating struggle to survive. Talk to most people and they will tell you about their financial problems, job problems, health problems, relationship problems, and the overall bad luck that plagues them. They feel fearful, insecure, and anxious. They are preoccupied with worry. In essence, they are not in control of their lives; their lives seem to be controlling them.

Life is a reflection of our own beliefs and points of view. Our beliefs literally shape our experience. If you think you are unlucky, a loser, things are happening to you, and life is unfair, you will be plagued by misfortune. Is it really bad luck, or are you just living out your beliefs? Perhaps you have had it all backward. You may have been dwelling on how unlucky you are and not realizing that your attitude is creating more bad luck. It may appear that we are victims of circumstances, but the truth is that we are the captain of our own ships and creators of our own destinies.

LIFE IS NOT FAIR—OR IS IT?

Some people spend half their life in hospitals while others are healthy. Some people spend their life in poverty, while others have more money than they know what to do with. On the surface, it seems that life is not fair. However, life is always fair because *things are the way they are.* What is unfair are our *expectations* of life. If you expect life to be fair based on your expectations of how people or situations are *supposed* to be, you will end up in the loony bin. (That's the clinical term for a psychiatric ward.) I can tell you right now: Life will always *appear* to be unfair.

In our personal lives, more often than not, things will not go as we expect and people will not live up to our expectations of what is fair or not fair. Often, the whole world appears to be chaotic. It will seem like those who should be rewarded are not rewarded, and those who should be punished are not punished. However, in studying quantum physics, we learn that most of what we see as disorder is actually chaotic order. Apparently random, unpredictable crisis, trauma, and destruction masks a higher order of events. Chaos, the actual process of disorder, is normal and natural.

Maintaining faith in apparent chaotic disorder is a major component in living a positive and productive life. This is not a form of blind faith or positive thinking, but an understanding that all breakthroughs and positive changes come from some form of meaningful chaos or disorder. When things don't go our way or life seems unfair, it is normal for us to ask three questions: Why me? Why now? What now?

Why Me?

It is normal to ask "Why me?" when things go wrong in our lives. Another variation of the question is "Why her?" or "Why him?" Many times we ask this in regard to a loved one, especially a child. Why does this have to happen to them? Why do they have to suffer so? Even when things go right, we ask, "Why me? Why is all this good stuff happening to me? Why am I having such good luck?" "Why do they have such good luck when they are such jerks?" The answer to the Why me? question is simply that *nothing is happening to us or them, it is just happening.* The problem is that we personalize it, as though it were happening to us.

A good illustration is a natural disaster. If a tornado strikes and your home is destroyed, you have an individual experience, but the tornado is not happening to you, it is just happening. Your experience of living through the destruction is your personalization of the event. Did you die? Obviously not, or you wouldn't be reading this book. Were you financially ruined forever? Probably not.

The library is filled with books about individuals rising out of despair. The despair caused them to change, and in retrospect they were thankful for their experience. It doesn't mean they would want to go through it again. It means that they have learned more about themselves and are stronger and wiser from the experience. The key is not to personalize every challenge or problem in life by assuming something is *happening* to you. Every time you ask "Why me?" you assume you are a victim of circumstances, people, or conditions. We need to keep reminding ourselves that things don't happen to *us* personally, they just happen, and the Why me? question only limits the possibility of finding a solution.

Why Now?

"Just when things were getting better." "Just when I was about to . . . this had to happen." "Why now?" Again, it is happening now, not just to us. If you are in a crowd and there is a gunshot and a bullet whizzes by you and misses you, is it happening to you? What about the person who gets shot? What about those who just hear a noise? Each person interprets or personalizes the event according to what happened to them. If a tree falls in the forest and you are not there, it's just falling. You can accept that. The tree is just falling. It is not happening to anyone. If, on the other hand, you walk under it while it is falling, you personalize it and say that the tree fell on you. You may ask, "Why me?" or "Why now?"

Fortunately, we cannot choose the time or nature of the traumas and crises in our lives. We can't tell the universe what to do, we can only be part of the events that unfold. The concept of time is irrelevant. Whenever anything happens to us, it is the perfect time for it to happen because it is happening. Our own personalized version of what we call the right or wrong time for it to happen is futile and irrelevant.

If you could schedule when a crisis or trauma was going to happen in your life, exactly what time would you select for damage to your marriage, relationship, child, career, home, financial security, or health? When is a good time for bad things to happen? The answer is obvious. There is no good time. As difficult as it is to accept, these things will happen, no matter how we feel about them and no matter how assiduously we try to avoid them.

What Now?

Our first reaction in a time of crisis is to try to do *something*— *anything*—to make it go away. We live in a culture that places an emphasis on immediate solutions to every problem. When something goes wrong in our lives, we feel the need to resolve our immediate situation by doing something. However, it is this very intensity and urgency to solve our problems that causes us to overlook permanent and lasting solutions.

Before we can resolve any problem, crisis, chaos, or trauma, we must learn from our experience so that we don't repeat it again. We must always keep in mind that *the lesson is more important than the solution.* If we just focus on an immediate solution, we will not learn the lesson and more than likely will encounter the same situation again some time in the future.

The "What do I do now?" question comes from our desire to put all the pieces of the puzzle together quickly without having any idea of what the entire puzzle looks like. Keep in mind that the picture of the puzzle is on the box so that you can see the end result before you begin sorting and putting together the pieces of the puzzle. In life, we also have to be able to see the end result (a permanent and lasting solution) before we can put the pieces together.

WHAT IS, IS WHAT IS

The study of quantum physics reveals to us that things do not just happen to us, they simply are. Everything that occurs in our lives is a series of events waiting for us to give them meaning by our perceptions. When we witness apparent chaos or destruction, are we viewing a universe, nation, or world out of control, or is infinite order being revealed to us through a temporary disruption? The important key is to understand that we cannot stop or redirect the flow of the universe or the way things are or what will happen. What we can do is observe what it is doing to us and how it effects change in our lives.

What about sickness? Is AIDS a punishment from God for our promiscuous behavior? Do we create sickness as some fields of psychology and metaphysics suggest? Or is sickness just a temporary physiological disruption of energy? What role does our genetic dice play in all this?

We must learn to see illness, destruction, trauma, and chaos not as a punishment from God or a predictor of doom, but as a temporary developmental adjustment. Most of all, we must learn to observe how we let it affect us and how we can change its effect upon us. There can be no healing without developmental adjustments.

Our impossible situations are influenced more by what we think than the way things are. Our perception of reality, which can be defined as *what is,* influences our behavior more than reality itself. Therefore, it's not the way things are that is the problem, but the way we *think* they are. Just because we think something is so does not mean that it is actually true. Perception forms everything in our life.

The problem with perception is that it not only influences the way things were and the way things are, but the way things will be in the future. It keeps us stuck because we spend so much time defending our perception. Our defense often borders on a pathological need to be right. When we spend most of our time and energy on being right or defending our position, we are unable to consider other options. Most of our energy is used up preparing our defense or rebuttal as to why thing are as they are and why we can't change. A worst-case scenario of this situation is if we have a life partner with the same perceptions. Now we have two people with a common goal based on the wrong perceptions.

Our perception of reality is formed from three sources: awareness, deletion, and distortion. *Awareness* is what we have been exposed to or programmed with from our outer and inner world. *Deletions* are those parts of reality that we have ignored or not experienced. It's like being tuned into a certain radio frequency and deleting all other frequencies. It doesn't mean that those frequencies do not exist, it just means we are not aware of them. *Distortion* is the filter through which we see reality. These are the assumptions that we make about things such as life, God, and what others are like. Our decisions and actions are based on these assumptions, which are often distorted through our filter of deletions (not having enough information). Distortions and deletions in turn influence our awareness of what is our reality.

Moving from the impossible to the possible requires that we modify our awareness. We can do this through conscious choice or it may be forced upon us as the result of events in our lives. We tend to look at things differently after a divorce, death, losing our money, failing a test, or losing our job or business. This gets our attention and alters our awareness. Whether we like it or not, these events are self-correcting and cause us to change our thinking and behavior.

What we are striving for is conscious awareness, awareness through choice. This is a conscious commitment to change our impossible situations to possible opportunities. *Our goal in life should be to convert what we know into positive results.* The measure of our decisions is if they serve us and others in a positive way. This is accomplished through *awareness and self-correction.*

WHAT? WELCOME PROBLEMS?

Since problems or seemingly impossible situations are inevitable, why not learn to welcome them instead of resisting them? They are *wake-up calls for creativity.* If we could almost welcome problems as they arise, seek the lesson before us early on, and make any changes or adjustments, we would experience less pain. The key is the perception we have of the problem. Is it such a bad problem, or do we make it worse in our minds? If the problem is very serious, can we handle it with strength like a master of life, or do we spend most of our energy trying to fight, ignore, or resist it?

As each opportunity or situation comes your way, remember that you have a choice to act on it in the best way you can. Every situation that you handle will be followed by another one. No matter how difficult things are, there is always the other side or *complementary opposite.* This is what we must look for, without denying where we are right now. We must accept our current reality and make the best of it.

PROBLEMS CAN SHIFT OUR COURSE
IN THE RIGHT DIRECTION

Problems often appear to be impossible situations. They signify our need to change something, usually ourselves. The problem is not what is important, it's what we do about it that makes all the difference.

Problems can motivate us to change and ultimately make things work better for ourselves and others. Some eastern philosophers, saints, and sages even see problems as life's gifts. Ancient sages say that the more problems we have, the more opportunities we have to raise our consciousness to that of a more highly developed person. After all, what you get by reaching your destination is not as important as what you become by reaching your destination. By any standards, our purpose on earth is to develop ourselves to the best of our abilities. Therefore, every problem or stumbling block that comes our way is a chance to change for the better.

WHAT WE LOOK FOR IS WHAT WE FIND

Our reality is created from our own observations. As unbelievable as it may seem, we see what we look for and create what we see. A psychologist using an ink blot test will ask patients what they see when they look at the ink blot. One patient may see a butterfly while another may see the face of the devil. A hungry person looking at a picture of a bowl of fruit will see it as a source of food; an artist may see it as a potential subject for a painting. What this teaches us is that we create our own reality by our own unique point of view.

Researchers know that what they discover is influenced by what they are looking for and who is doing the looking. Repeated and double-blind experiments in which researchers are unaware of what is being studied are often used to control the influence of the observer creating the results of the experiment. Extending this idea into daily life, what we see actually creates what we experience as individuals, couples, families, communities, states, nations, and the world.

Why do we tend to see the glass as half empty, rather than the glass being half full? When we get into negative thinking, we often see only the problems we face instead of looking for the good we can find. The question to ask ourselves is, How often does this happen to me? How can we minimize our negative thoughts? When we introspect, self-observe, we can notice more intently how we respond to different situations. Then we can create a change in our thinking by realizing what our mind is doing and by choosing to look for the solutions to our problems, or even find golden opportunities within our problems.

LIVING WITH UNCERTAINTY

One of the things that scares most people is living in uncertainty. You cannot identify one aspect of your life that is totally certain. Even when you will die or what may follow is uncertain. At best, it remains a matter of speculation.

Unfortunately, most people would rather be certain of something that is uncertain. They would rather accept a point of view that they have never verified for themselves than live with uncertainty. This is the foundation of all religions.

RELIGION—OUR ULTIMATE SEARCH
FOR CERTAINTY

Religion satisfies our need for certainty. Regardless of the teachings of any religion, none can offer proof that what it teaches is the truth. The only proof is in the sacred books, writings, and revelations given exclusively to each religion by God. And, of course, each one is different. What religious teachers ask of followers is to substitute lack of proof with faith. The problem is that *we see what we look for and believe what we find.*

The Wayfare Institute is comprised of some of the finest biblical scholars from several universities and theological schools. Over the past twelve years, these scholars have been studying the Bible from a secular point of view. The project is called the Jesus Seminar. This group has approached the Bible from a strictly *historical* point of view. The goal, unlike that in traditional theology, is not to prove that everything in the Bible is true, but to set aside only those teachings that could be historically verified. The discoveries were quite interesting.

The scholars found that only 20 percent of what is written in the New Testament can be verified as the actual teachings of Jesus. That includes most of what Jesus was supposed to have said. If these findings are correct, that could blow the lid off the fundamental theory that the Bible is the exact word of God. Those who have a need for certainty will be the most threatened by the conclusions of this study because it attacks the very foundations of their beliefs.

Challenging our beliefs is always healthy, because it brings us to a new level of awareness. *If we think we know, we don't.* Only when we are willing to admit that there is a possibility that we don't know, can we grow and learn more of the truth. This comes through living in uncertainty.

COMPLEMENTARY OPPOSITES—
LOOKING AT THE WHOLE

There are complementary sides to every aspect of our existence. The concept of complementary opposites teaches us that there is an opposite side to everything. Up and down, good and bad, front and back, positive and negative are all connected. We tend to see things as disjointed, yet our reality is composed of parts of a greater picture. Unfortunately, we tend to believe that the part we see is the whole. Our intellectual and emotional conditioning, which includes compartmentalization of reality, prevents us from seeing the whole picture. Most perceptions are divorced from the total context.

Imagery, meditation, mind over matter, and positive thinking all have their place, but permanent and lasting change comes from changing our perception of our situation. We must allow for discomfort and then realize that it can be changed, if we will make changes. Often we have to have greater discomfort or pain from our current situation than the amount of pain we think is involved in making the change before we are willing to make the change. Simply put, when it becomes more difficult to suffer than change, you will change.

CHANGE ON A DIME, GAIN NINE

Remember the phrase, "A stitch in time saves nine"? How about, "Change in time, makes things fine"? Why not change sooner, before the difficulty intensifies? Obviously, we would spare ourselves from an unnecessary extension of pain if we would change sooner rather than later. If we become paralyzed and afraid to make a move for fear that another problem will come along, then we remain stuck in our fears. Of course, there will be more problems. That's the way life goes. If we maintain a positive frame of mind, we are more likely to fill the new space with positive experiences. This is especially so if we have learned from our past mistakes.

If we have not learned from the last experience, a similar experience will come along so we will have a chance to try again to get the message. Life is a persistent teacher. It will keep repeating lessons until we learn.

GOING BEYOND POSITIVE
THINKING

When illness, crisis, or trauma enters our lives, we are told to adopt a positive attitude. Although this may seem logical on the surface, we must allow ourselves to feel depressed, helpless, and angry. These are important feelings, just as are happiness and joy. The principle of complementary opposites teaches us that there is an opposite aspect to everything. Up and down, happy and sad, and hope and despair are all important aspects of a healthy personality.

The individual who is always positive often uses it as a way to cover up unpleasant feelings such as anger, sadness, worry, and depression. This person is just as psychologically imbalanced as the person who overindulges in these negative feelings. Real life is about feeling the ups and the downs and knowing that there is something good and positive to be found during our feelings of sadness or disappointment. How else can we contemplate different ways to look at situations and then make positive changes and improvements in our direction?

Although it may be a bit uncomfortable to clearly review something unfavorable that has happened in our lives, some of the best decisions we ever make are realized in times of crisis. We all have our breaking point and it is OK if we reach it at some times in our lives. We must acknowledge such feelings and let them happen in order to work through them and rise again in a most triumphant way, allowing what we learned to lift us to new heights.

It has been said that some people wear rose-colored glasses. They might be overdoing their positive outlook on life to the point of being unrealistic and are in danger of overlooking important pitfalls to avoid. However, there are times when putting on rose-colored glasses can be appropriate, after our tears have been shed, when it is time to move on to new and better horizons.

Balancing between these complementary opposites is like a dance, and the dance becomes easy when we understand what we can do with the insight we gain from the dance. We can direct our lives on the best track for ourselves with such powerful insight.

Without such insight, we fail to see clearly where we are and where we want to go. If we don't know where we are, we surely cannot sail our ship in the right direction.

What do you think happens over your lifetime if you don't correct your false beliefs? Over time, how far off course do you think that might take you? Look at your life right now. Are you on course? Imagine what it is going to be like in the next five or ten years. How satisfying will it be then if your life isn't the way you want it because you didn't make the necessary corrections?

RESISTANCE

We resist for a variety of reasons, which may include deep-seated negative psychological programming by those who influenced us in our childhood, fear of the unknown, fear of failure, fear of being judged by others, having a fixed or rigid perspective, or being very uncomfortable when we simply change a habit. Notice I said *simply* change a habit, but try writing with your opposite hand and see how weird it feels. Not so simple, eh? Some people even remain in lousy relationships because they are more comfortable with what is familiar and known, even though it is often painful.

We know we should change, but we tend to resist change with every fiber of our being. Whatever we resist persists and often intensifies, so why do we resist? Even as you read this chapter, you are probably experiencing resistance at some level. Your mind may be telling you that what you are reading is true, but it doesn't apply to you, because in your case, it's different. I'm sorry, my friend, but it's the same for all of us. The harder you resist, the harder it is to break through the impossible to the possible. In effect, we become our own worst enemies. It's like shooting ourselves in the foot each time we tell ourselves that something is impossible.

We all have our own behavioral comfort zones. There is a part of us that wants to change and move to the edge of the circle, and there is a part of us that wants to stay in the middle, isolated from change. Think about anything you have done. Part of you wanted to do it, and part of you fought change. The problem with staying in the middle is that we continue to do more of what we have been doing in order to maintain the status quo. The more we tend to stay in the middle of the circle, the more we close off our options.

Some of us hold on tightly, even fiercely, to our foundation of beliefs, fearing that to change our views would destroy our foundation. Our minds are not like pyramids, where if you take a piece out from the bottom, all the rest will tumble down. Yes, we should hold on to our thoughts and robustly convey them in a debatable situation, but we must also change on a dime when someone gives us a new piece of information or a new concept that warrants a change in our view. This is the greatest strength of character of all. Greater is this strength than being one of the ones who builds their little stockpile while they think they are set for life and in control. Life can bring us some small pebbles to deal with, or life's ebbs and flows can bring us a bowling ball that surely will make that pyramid tumble down.

Doesn't it seem like these bowling balls or giant boulders come rolling into our lives when we have some kind of great lesson to learn? Usually we figure this out after the unsettling experience has forced us to reach new heights, to break through our set ways. Perhaps life brings us more bowling balls when we build stockades around us in our attempts to have certainty and security.

Fear of the unknown can get in the way of our greatest life experiences or hinder the greatest results we can achieve. If we hold on to our foundation of knowledge with so much scrutiny that little can reach us, we are limited by our conscious mind. We hear so often that scientific experts say that we do not use all of our brains. To reach farther within our minds, we need to go beyond what we know or what we think we know. Our conscious mind knows what we know, such as how to cook or change a tire on our car, but the subconscious mind knows so much more. It knows *all* that we have ever heard or seen, although we think we do not remember these things. Everything we have ever heard or seen can be remembered. We just need to reach it through techniques, such as using mental exercises, relaxation techniques, or physical exercise.

Our conscious mind knows what we know and it is aware of those things we don't know (such as, I don't know how to write a computer program). We tend to think we do not know things that are merely buried in our subconscious minds somewhere because we cannot seem to retrieve them at the moment. Actually, we are capable of retrieving any information within our minds. Sometimes we may think a thought is an original one, when it actually may have entered our minds from some other source at some other time.

When we come up with truly original ideas, the genius in us comes to the fore. We are tapping universal knowledge, where Einstein grasped his brilliant ideas. This occurs when we have reached our superconscious minds. Our superconscious minds are our power centers, and they *know the perfect way* for us, a realm of absolute ideas that *cannot be wrong*. This source, which we can contact at will, always gives us the information we need to lead us out of barren places into more productive fields. William James called this transcendental power the *superconscious mind.* Emerson referred to it as the *universal mind.* Whatever you call it, just believe that it *does* exist and, because it always knows the perfect way for you, that you can tap its unlimited potential to receive the creative ideas you need to solve your problems.

HOW TO REMAIN OPEN TO IDEAS

When it comes to knowing and not knowing, wouldn't it be best for us to quickly admit that we don't know something and then seek ideas that are deep within our minds or that come from great inspiration? How about having the gumption to just let someone else contribute an idea?

We can always increase our listening ability. Then we could grasp so much more available intelligence. Listening to ourselves, listening to all the wonderful minds of others, and listening by observation, where we notice important subtle images that are all around us gives us *unlimited resources.* We could save ourselves a lot of time and trouble by learning from other people's experiences.

Do you build mental roads by which you can meet and share yourself with other people, or do you erect mental walls that separate you from others? These walls can never stand against time and change, but if you build roads that join you to other people, you can travel endlessly through time. You can change the direction of your course and make your resources virtually unlimited. These roads can be lifelines, like arteries to the hearts, minds, and souls of others with all their wisdom becoming yours as well. You will be empowered with this kind of strength, rather than be a stone wall that is actually superficial and is easily broken down.

You can resist change by saying, "I can't help it. That's just the way I am!" The truth is, whatever is happening in your life right now is not determined by the way you are but by the way you have chosen to be.

Rest assured, life's problems and challenges will confront you. You can perceive your problems as breaking you down, or you can perceive the experiences as challenges that are building you up and carrying you away in a much better direction in the long run.

IS SOMETHING REALLY GOING WRONG, OR IS IT REALLY GOING RIGHT?

Life is filled with uncertainty, but we must trust that there is truly some kind of divine order that is right for us. Usually, something that is going wrong is really going to make things go right in the long run. We often can't see the forest for the trees until we have walked all the way through it.

Under most circumstances, we are not able to see what lies ahead. Looking back, we can see how impossible situations that seemed to be going wrong actually worked to our benefit. Very few of us have the ability to accurately look into the future. None of us knows for sure what the future may bring. But we must know that whatever happens, there is always a reason and a solution. The reason may or may not be apparent, but the solution is available if we trust that we have the inner power to handle any situation.

Each failure brings you closer to success. If you allow failure and rejection to run your life, you will severely limit your possibilities. Keep in mind that you have an equal chance to succeed in anything if you will just give it a chance. You have nothing to lose until you give up.

RESPONSE TO PROBLEMS— POSSIBILITY VS. IMPOSSIBILITY

Each time we are faced with a problem, we have two choices. We can perceive the problem as a threat and fear it, or we can perceive the problem as an opportunity to meet a challenge. We can go into distress, or we can feel a positive level of stress—the kind of tension that gives us just the right amount of adrenaline to feel the thrill of overcoming the problem. However, we block this rush of positive adrenaline when we block the positive energy-boosting emotions. Our western culture encourages us to not feel emotions, but to be logical. Using only logical, linear, left-brain thinking eliminates our dynamic sense of challenge, adventure, empowerment, and victory. Some people are so logical that they don't even enjoy a victorious outcome, no matter which road they took to get there.

If we are consumed with self-doubt, fear, or anger by perceiving problems as threats to our survival, we are just allowing ourselves to be engulfed with the feeling that we have no control and that things are *happening to us*. As soon as we are faced with trouble, we should evaluate our attitudes and perception, looking to see if we are feeling like a victim, and immediately turn around the problem by looking for possibilities and viewing them as opportunities and challenges.

LETTING GO OF WHAT DOESN'T WORK

One of the most difficult obstacles we face in changing the impossible to the possible is letting go of what doesn't work. We tend to remain in jobs and careers we dislike, we don't deal with unresolved conflict, we don't love as passionately as we want, we replay negative experiences in our mind, we practice unhealthy physical patterns, we remain bored or scared, and we are afraid to change. On top of all this, we reinforce our impossible situations by telling our troubles to anyone who will listen.

Even though our past behaviors are causing pain, we keep doing the same thing over and over again. This is a form of mental illness. One of the characteristics of mentally ill people is that they repeatedly do the same thing but expect different results. Said another way, if you keep doing what you have been doing, you will keep getting what you have been getting. Instead of changing, we manifest the immobilization behaviors of inaction: we promise to change in the future, but we continue to repeat strategies that don't work. This not only limits our ability to make the impossible possible but generates inner stress.

Our unwillingness or inability to change is rooted in our decision that something out there is preventing us. To justify our position, we form a victim mentality that essentially says that what is happening to us is not our fault. If "they" (parents, family, boss, mate, or government) were not standing in our way, we could have what we want. This victim mentality of blaming, criticizing, rationalizing, justifying, explaining, avoiding, and attempting to change external forces keeps us trapped in impossible life situations. As we empower these outside forces, our options become fewer. In turn, this self-limiting process prevents us from using our creative resources to work through our self-created obstacles. As long as we blame others, we remain ignorant about our contribution to the problem or what we can do to change it. Blame always involves giving up power.

LEARNING THE LESSON, THROWING AWAY THE EXPERIENCE

Most of the impossible situations we experience are a product of our past choices, not our circumstances. The sum total of our life is linked to the choices we have made. As stated earlier, things don't just happen to us. However, not all of our choices are made out of conscious awareness. Many times we are just operating out of false beliefs and values.

It is amazing that we can survive all this, since some of the consequences can throw our life into chaos or even be dangerous. For many people, life is not a matter of living, it is just a matter of surviving the consequences of their choices. The downside is, if we survive the consequences of our choices, we are less likely to change. Instead, we accept the consequences of our poor choices while living life in the survival mode. Success, happiness, and inner joy, however, cannot be experienced if we are living in the survival mode.

Every choice we make either moves us closer or farther away from where we want to be. All progress in life, whether individually or collectively, comes through the power of choice. We can either choose to stay in the past or move into the future. Most of the time, the solution is within us, but we just don't act on it. The law of inertia comes into play. It is more difficult to get a standing object moving than one that has a little momentum.

Finding yourself in impossible situations can be turned into a positive experience. Consider it a breakthrough opportunity or a wake-up call that will enable you to move from where you are to where you want to be. We must begin by replacing the thought pattern of, "That's the way it is meant to be," or "That's the way I am," with "Up until now, that's the way I was," or "Up until now, that the way it was."

When we go through difficult times and finally resolve our problem, we need to keep the lesson but throw away the experience. In other words, focus on what you learned from *solving* your problem rather than what *happened* to you. Instead of playing over and over what they did, what they said, how they did it to you, or how life was unfair, focus on the solution and how you can *avoid* this type of problem again. Realize that you are now much wiser and more capable of handling similar problems if they should arise.

By taking the initiative to change our destiny, we break the cycle of repeating our past experiences over and over again. The moment we determine we are the cause and not the effect, we gain power to control our destiny. If we don't, history will just keep repeating itself until we get the lesson.

MIRACLES—FACT OR MYTH?

Are there such things as miracles? What are miracles, anyway? Let's go back to the Why me? Why now? What now? scenario. Picture two parents in a hospital emergency room. Both have a child who may die at any moment from a serious illness. Both pray to God, asking him to spare their child. One child lives and the other dies. The question we must ask is, did God allow one to live and the other to die, or is that just the way it is?

As always, we have a choice in our perception. Whenever we don't understand something, we call it a miracle. And, of course, miracles are always positive. When something goes wrong, it is not a miracle; instead, it is fate or bad luck. Keep in mind that at one time in our history, it would have been a miracle to see an airplane in the sky because no one knew about aerodynamics. Many of the things we take for granted today would have been amazing miracles during the life span of Jesus. The unexplainable is often viewed as a miracle until we know the principle behind it.

Miracles are not God breaking his rules. Miracles are evidence of our conscious or unconscious acceptance of what is happening at the moment based on a principle or universal law of which we have no knowledge. The more we learn about the way things are, the more we realize that there are no miracles, only perfect order where everything is happening to the right person at the right time in the right way, based on our level of awareness as individuals, countries, and nations.

No matter what we are facing, we must realize that the problem or apparent bad luck is only a *temporary* situation. Once we have the answer to our problem and act on it, we can change it from a negative experience to a positive one. It is at that moment that so-called miracles will occur.

CHAPTER 2

The Greater Self
and the Created Self

HUMAN SPIRIT—THE GREATER SELF

Where did you come from? When confronted with that question, most of us would answer, "From my parents." However, your parents had parents, too, and if we continue to look back in time, we see that life flows from a continuous line of creation. If we ask where did the creation come from, we have no answer but that of the one creator or universal substance. If this is so, then we come from the one substance or creator. In other words, our life is born *through* our parents not *of* our parents.

This line of thought leads us to the conclusion that we are much more than we appear. This essence of who we really are is the *Created Self*, because it came from and was created by the one creator. When we think of ourselves as single individuals, we lose sight of our true power. It is this feeling of separation from who we really are, the Created Self, that is the seed of impossibility thinking. Instead of focusing on who we are, we must focus on *what we have become*, which is our Created Self.

Perhaps you have heard of the 100th monkey phenomenon. In the late 1970s, the Japanese government studied a small colony of monkeys that lived on several adjoining islands in the Philippines. While observing the behavior of the monkeys, they noticed that one monkey had discovered how to clean dirt from potatoes by washing them in a stream. The monkey taught this skill to several other monkeys, one at a time. After the 100th monkey had been taught, something very strange happened. Every monkey in the entire colony was instantly able to perform this same skill without being taught. When the number reached 100, it apparently made a quantum leap of consciousness because every monkey was able to perform this skill. This seems to support the *one mind* concept.

Our perception of oneness can be viewed as a universe with one mind, but with billions of individual brains that contribute to the whole, rather than billions of individual brains all going in separate directions. We share the one mind and consciousness with everything and everyone around us, including animals and plants. The Greater Self is an extension and expression of the infinite one mind, which may be called by many different names, such as *spirit*, the *Earth Mother, God, the force,* or just *energy.*

If we understand that our Greater Self came from and is one with the universal substance, we must then ask why the universal substance gave us life. Why are we here? Are we to be born without a way to understand the meaning of our lives? Are we to spend the rest of our lives eating, sleeping, working, trying to entertain and amuse ourselves, and then die without knowing the purpose of our existence? I don't think so.

ASSETS AND LIABILITIES

Businesses take an annual inventory of profits and losses, assets and liabilities, what is working and what isn't. Depending on how much we are working on ourselves or changing ourselves, we should take inventory with some kind of regularity as well. An inventory of our liabilities might include personality defects such as intolerance, dishonesty, pride, procrastination, fear, or selfishness, but a personal inventory is not about assessing only our liabilities. We can't leave out the *assets* in an *assessment.*

An inventory does not have to be a lengthy list of all that is wrong with us, but rather a look at our assets, uniqueness, strengths, weaknesses, or areas we want to improve. Most importantly, the elements of our personal inventory need to be of such a nature that we can measure and review our progress. If we see a problem repeating itself in a pattern, it will make it easier for us to stop the pattern by recognizing the scenario that triggers the habitual behavior. Wouldn't taking an honest look at your life and taking a personal inventory help you achieve your Greater Self and your greatest happiness? Wouldn't it help you eliminate your old, undesirable self, which was created by others' expectations, and encourage development of a new, Greater Self?

Build your assets, even turn your liabilities into assets, then your Greater Self will be fully realized. One way to explore and heighten your assets is to examine them through your purpose, which is your passion. You see, not only does purpose give you strength, it also rallies your talents to the fore. If you are doing a worthwhile thing, then you appreciate your true strengths, skills, and talents. By becoming aware of your strengths, you feel more complete, whole, and naturally motivated. It feels so much better to do what you want to do rather than what you feel burdened to do. If you are using the talents that give you pleasure, you will no longer be looking outside yourself for happiness, because your work and recreation will be fully satisfying.

If you ask yourself how you could be excited about doing certain jobs, then let me tell you about a Roto-Rooter serviceman's story that was shown on a television news magazine show. The episode was about how customer service is perceived in America these days, where the public is getting so used to poor service that they no longer expect good service. The television show featured a man who was exuberant about his work, even though his job of fixing messed-up sewage systems could get pretty funky. His attitude was marvelous. He was skilled, with many years of experience, and most importantly, he was *outstanding*.

His uniqueness stood out. He was incredibly positive with his customers and he would go above and beyond the call of duty by doing something like cleaning up not only what mess he may have made, but also the surrounding mess that existed before he got there. The special effort he put into cleaning up was actually an easy extra step, but the customers noticed it and loved it. This man did more. His van contained endless unique, self-created devices he used to achieve excellence in his work, such as having cologne, mirrors, and even a shower so that he could clean himself up between customers.

The list could go on and on with this Roto-Rooter serviceman's unique ideas, which demonstrated the quality of his work and, most of all, his pride and enthusiasm for his job. The man was literally radiant because he knew he was worth something, worth something grand, even though he works with sewage. And guess what! He earns $70,000 per year! If he thinks he's worth something, what do you think you are worth? You will never let yourself have more money than you think you are worth.

Another individual named Peter Franklin, who has a seemingly ordinary job, has reached the big time by being an extraordinary individual. Franklin is a cabby who is aired all over the world as a talk radio personality. He broadcasts his wisdom from his cab while driving the crazy streets of New York. How did he get noticed? By his radiant personality, which expressed his greatest self, of course. He is quite a character. How is your character?

If you see yourself as your best or Greater Self, identify all your most motivating talents, and rally them toward some issue or interest you care about, then you will create work environments that truly fit who you really are, even while working at a job that is unsuited to your greatest talents and abilities. You will be happy and fulfilled when you choose to let go, and let your *real* self out.

Personal change always seems difficult, if not impossible, as long as we are focused on what we don't have (liabilities) as opposed to what we do have going for us (assets). The first step is taking a look at our assets rather than our liabilities. Assets are the tools in our favor that we can use to make the impossible possible. The more we focus on our assets, the more power we will have to change our life and circumstances. Let's take a look at some of our assets.

Spiritual Assets

Belief or lack of belief in a connection to a higher power (whatever you believe it to be) can be a spiritual asset or a spiritual liability. It is important to understand that we are spiritual beings with a temporary human experience, not human beings with a temporary spiritual experience. What this means is that you will outlive and outlast anything that is going on in your life right now. Whether you are tall, short, thin, fat, heterosexual, homosexual, Asian, Caucasian, European, African, male, female, rich, poor, sick, or healthy, this is only your temporary state of being. To a large extent, you have control of this temporary state. Who *you are*—your Greater Self or human spirit—is permanent and lasting. What is important to understand is that what you have and what you do is only temporary.

Your perception of who you are mentally, physically, and spiritually forms your Greater Self. This Greater Self is a composite of principles, values, decisions, experiences, friends, heroes, suffering, passion, habits, visions, beliefs, dreams, realities, and goals that are tied to your purpose. Your Greater Self is driven by your life purpose.

Regardless of whether we are clear about our purpose on earth, we can be clear about what we decide to contribute to the world and ourselves. If you have a passion to serve mankind, then this purpose can be tied to what work you choose to do. If your purpose is tied to what surrounds you, such as you and your family, then your purpose in doing the work that you do is to provide for your family. Nonetheless, there is a *purpose* behind every goal. In other words, earning a certain amount of money per year is your goal, but your purpose is to create the life you want. Purpose is what motivates you toward your goals. Therefore, your passion and your spirit are what compel you. Expressing your passion motivates you to be fully engaged in your work and life.

Your reason for doing whatever you do can be specifically tied to your goals in your job, even if your job may be somewhat mundane compared to your worldly concerns. For example, if a business is marketing an item to a certain group of consumers, the purpose behind any goals the company sets is to provide the best product that will make their customers more satisfied, so that people will prefer their products over some other companies' products. Companies who are clear about the purpose of their products and their customers' *reasons* for using their products will surpass companies whose product designers are simply competing among themselves for what appears to be the best idea. Having a clear purpose keeps us on track in the right direction and motivates us with a passion.

The human element can never be left out of business. This is why businesses seek innovation from the spirit and passion of their employees. They know that without it, their businesses could not survive and thrive in these highly competitive times. Individually, your passion and spirit make you the best you can be. Your uniqueness is what makes you a valuable contribution to any purpose or organization. Your Greater Spirit is your asset. Your purpose is your innermost self desiring to express itself. You will be happy if you are engaged in what you do.

Values Align Your Purpose with Your Goals

Purpose brings us clarity about where we are going and what specifically we are doing on a daily basis in order to accomplish that end. Commitment to a purpose larger than ourselves gives us meaning. Purpose makes us feel inspired and empowered. We feel like there is always something we can do that can make a difference. Purpose toward something larger is what has driven the great achievers of the world. The larger picture is never merely about larger amounts of money, it is about what we value.

One of the most successful Hollywood talent agents and movie producers, David Geffin, cited this quote in a recent television interview. "The man who says money will make him happy doesn't have money." David Geffin is known to have more money than most people in Hollywood. He worked his way up in his field from being an usher at a television studio to representing some of the greatest names in Hollywood and the world (such as Elton John), and most recently has formed a movie studio that is equal in stature to MGM or 20th Century Fox. Geffin has all the money and success he could possibly want, and yet he chooses to continue to work hard, take risks, and pursue intense challenges.

Early on, Geffin realized his passion for television and the movies, attracted by the powerful effect these media had on people. He realized it was his passion from his first job as an usher for television audiences in the early days of black-and-white TV. From there, he worked in the mail room at the William Morris talent agency. He was flexible and able to make changes quickly when he saw opportunities. When he saw one of the agents in action on the telephone one day, he thought he could do what he saw, and achieved this goal within the agency. Later, he built his own top-drawer talent agency. David Geffin did not know how great he would eventually become. He did not set goals that were unrealistic. He simply kept working in the field that was his passion and became great by his own dynamics. Geffin said that, at first, he had no vision beyond making $1,000 per week and wanting a certain car that he dreamed of. In a television interview he said, "There's God's plan, and there's your plan, and your plan doesn't matter."

Geffin felt that he was carried along his career path by his passion and dedication to his work. He certainly fulfilled all he committed himself to doing most effectively. Although he worked hard on tasks and goals on a daily basis, he did not set out to be the greatest film producer. Instead, he became a great film producer as a result of his accomplishments as a passionate and productive individual. Money was not his top priority; his work was.

Ancient wisdom tells us that if our desires are based too much on material things because we want to have more than others, then we may become easily frustrated and angry when we do not get what we want. Those who have visions of grandeur and yet hold those visions with good values and good pleasure can enjoy themselves while they journey toward their ideals. Having a wholesome view, filled with dreams of enjoyment, enshrouds us with more happiness all along the way.

This is not to say that hard work isn't necessary. At times, we might have to muster up every ounce of our strength to get what we want. There are times when we might need to be like a warrior, fighting to get where we want to go. Only we can know which methods are best at any given time on our journey or mission. Purpose generates strength and courage around our deepest satisfactions.

If our desires are also based on winning, and in turn defeating others, we lose the depth of meaning and strength we need to conduct ourselves successfully and happily. For example, people who are too involved in winning during a sticky divorce will exhaust themselves in the battle rather than turn over matters to professionals who can more competently handle all the problems. We must certainly take care of overseeing critical details, but we can destroy our happiness by thinking that our value is about winning, which includes an emphasis on defeating others.

Is Your Life about Meaning or Matter?

Is your life about being a consumer? There is little time for meaning when your life is spent in getting, consuming, fixing, repairing, and maintaining physical matter that you cannot take with you when you leave this planet.

Unfortunately, most of us have little understanding of how valuable it would be for us to have meaning in all we do. We should ask ourselves, "Why am I doing this?" "What do I want to accomplish?" "Why is this task more important than another?" "Why is this person approaching me?" The last question is a good one to ask yourself often, or to ask the person who is approaching you with conversation, especially if he or she rambling. What a time saver.

You don't have to have a crisis in order to make more meaningful choices in directing your life. A university study of sixty students who had attempted suicide were asked why they did so. Eighty-five percent stated that their reason was because their life seemed meaningless. Surprisingly, 93 percent of the students were having good social and family relationships, and they were doing well academically. Viktor Frankl has said, "Ever more, people today have the means to live, but no meaning to live for." When our lives have meaning we are not just enduring life and surviving, rather we will hold an enduring light of true satisfaction and happiness.

The only thing we can take with us is the knowledge or meaning we have given to our lives. The matter, the physical stuff, must be left behind. Our focus should be on those things that will be with us forever. Relationships, love, helping one another, creating a better world, and cooperating with the perfect pattern of our unfoldment as extensions of the one mind as our Greater Self has infinite value.

Mental Assets

Mental assets include our attitudes, perception, knowledge, problem-solving ability, and style of thinking (linear vs. creative thinking, which is right-brain/left-brain thinking). It is no great secret that by controlling our thoughts we can control our attitudes. This is the single greatest asset because attitude determines action. Our attitudes determine whether we are going to be depressed or enthusiastic, whether we are going to take responsibility or complain and blame others. The choice is always ours and ours alone. No one can influence an individual's attitude. We are the ones who ultimately decide what we are going to think and those thoughts form our attitudes about who we are and what we are capable of accomplishing. This is why the capacity for choosing our thoughts is our greatest power.

People go to therapists for weeks, months, and years only to find out that if they change their perception, they can change their thinking. If they change their thinking, they can change their attitudes. If they change their attitudes or outlook, they can change their outer experiences. You can save yourself all that expensive therapy by coming to the same conclusion and accepting this truth.

Rediscover your true self by reviewing all of your feelings, hopes, fears, desires, and values to find out what matters to you, not what matters to someone else or what matters to certain groups of people. Not only are we creatures of habit, but we are creatures of social habits, and social habitats. There are times when others' judgments will, if we allow them, creep into our behavior. The more you honestly and clearly explore yourself in relation to your inner desires and values, the more self-directed your life will be. To a great degree, you can control your own destiny if you are not afraid to take risks.

Rolling the Dice, Taking Risks

If we think of life as a game, we surely have to take some risks, or we will not get anywhere on the playing board. Life is fair; the game is fair. All is perfect in the end. This you will see by just welcoming, or at least accepting, what comes your way and openly and honestly looking at what is really happening to you, and most of all seeing the purpose of things, the reason why everything happens as it does. The reason why unpleasant things happen is not because you personally deserve misfortune or unhappiness because you're no good. There are two reasons why such things happen. One is because we must make a change that we may be resisting, and the other is found in the beauty of the lesson we can learn from the experience.

As the song goes, "For every season, there is a reason, and a time for every purpose under heaven." The word *purpose* and the answer to the word *why* are almost synonymous. It is funny though, that as children we may have often been told not to ask why so much. Yet asking why of yourself and others more often could be quite interesting. For example, just asking a person, "Why did you call?" especially if that person is rambling, could make your time and the time of the caller much more efficient. Asking yourself why you are working on one thing rather than another can make a difference in setting priorities in your time management.

"But," you might ask, "if everything has a reason, why would we lose a loved one?" There is always a reason. It may have been best for that person to go on elsewhere, whether you like it or not. After all, who said this world is paradise? Some wonderful people are only here for a short time, or what seems like a short time. Why were they taken from us so early? Why then, would a wicked person be given a long life? Who knows? Since we can't change what happens to us, our only choice for sound mental and spiritual health is to change how we *feel* about what happens. This is something we have control over.

Physical Assets

In order to actualize our thoughts, we must be able to take *physical action* at the appropriate time. This is accomplished through physical energy, movement, sex drive, health, strength, stamina, and fitness. If we are not in balance in any of these areas, we will sabotage our success because we will have to compensate for lacking in these areas of physical well-being.

Motivation is a combination of physical energy and mental energy. Actually, since the mind controls our physical body, it is our minds that truly drive us to take any action. If our attitude is negative, we won't be motivated to go anywhere or do anything. Motivation is having a good attitude about doing things we may not always *feel* like doing. When our purpose and passion are tied into our mind-set, we'll do almost anything to get where we want to go. Finally, all we need to do is *believe* in what we are doing. We can enable this to happen when we realize that we will do almost anything it takes to get what we want.

Only you can motivate yourself. No one can be motivated by others. The important factor is that you are motivated to do the most positive and constructive activities rather than destructive activities, such as laziness. To overcome negative motivation, it is essential that you change your awareness of what you desire and how you can achieve it. Once you focus your desires, you will be motivated to do the right thing for yourself. You must be convinced that any change you make will bring about the gratification of a particular need or desire.

Your motivation can be elevated by increasing your awareness of the potential benefits of taking any given action. People can attempt to motivate you, they can even threaten you, but unless you desire to make changes and take actions for which you can see rewards, you will not do it, no matter what the consequences might be. Without being aware of and in touch with your positive inner desires, you could sabotage your own success by making the wrong choices due to lazy and self-destructive motivation.

The criminal, alcoholic, overeater, or drug addict have all gone through the same process and, based on their levels of awareness, decided that addiction is worth whatever price they have to pay for it. Once their awareness changes—usually under tragic circumstances—they realize that the cost of *escaping* from reality and a self they have come to hate is too high for what they are receiving in return. Their motivation then sets them on a more positive course.

People can only change through their own conscious decisions. Until their awareness is changed, people will not do what *you* want them to do. You can try every method of coercement, you can even try to scare them into action, but their action will only be temporary in order to get you off their backs. People will only change when they align their passion and spirit, setting their motivation in gear toward their own positive vision.

Skills Assets

Along with our personal inventory, we need to review our specific skills in relation to the work we are doing and our basic professional skills, such as communications and interpersonal skills. Make a checklist of your skills and particularly note which areas of expertise you have not brushed up on lately. Continuing education is vital. There is always more to learn, yet we tend to think we know it all.

How are you at handling conflicts, negotiating, persuading, giving directions that someone else can clearly understand, building partnerships and team mates, prioritizing, time managing, and making decisions? Many people do not realize that there are actually seminars specifically on the subject of decision making. Have you ever taken a course in decision making? How about an entire course on listening skills?

If you want to double-check to see what skills you might enhance, take a look at a good role model and see what that person does. Ask the role model questions, and then pursue the skills and techniques he or she uses. Have you ever asked someone if you could spend a day with him or her to find out how that person functions? This is not something just for students to do; a seasoned professional can do so and, if anything, you will actually impress the person you are interviewing.

The Asset of Persistence with Flexibility

Persistence receives the category of being an asset on its own. The following quote of President Calvin Coolidge says it all:

> Nothing in the world can take the place of persistence. Talent will not. Nothing is more common than unsuccessful men with talent. Genius will not. Unrewarded genius is almost a proverb. Education will not. The world is full of educated derelicts. Persistence and determination alone are omnipotent. The slogan "press on" has solved, and always will solve, the problems of the human race.

Although the essence and drive of persistence is the bottom line in accomplishing great things, being persistent to the point of ignorance and stubbornness is just plain stupid. And disappointingly, we see people and businesses resist adjusting their plan because they think they will lose their plan altogether. The internationally renowned business advisor and syndicated columnist, Tom Peters, who wrote *In Search of Excellence,* also wrote another best-seller called *Thriving on Chaos.* Peters elaborates throughout his books that flexibility and quickness are keys to success in these fast-paced times. Nonetheless, the key here is the balance between action and inaction, knowing when to hold 'em and when to fold 'em.

During my first efforts as an entrepreneur, I constantly examined my capabilities by observing myself and measuring myself against all the qualities I needed to be successful. Among all the quotes relating to excellence, I found persistence to be key. I could keep reviewing my marketing plan, business plan, resources of products and suppliers, performance style, office management, on and on, but the key was persistence. I needed the persistence to perform most consistently the tasks that brought me income, and it was important to realize that I should not get too caught up in perfecting my accounting system, computer system, or what have you, instead. As much as the systems appeared to be important, there was no comparison to the critical importance of getting these nonproductive tasks out of the way and performing the tasks that brought real revenue. Sounds like simple prioritizing, but once you get caught up in managing a business, you can easily lose critical production time that brings you income. Entrepreneurs start wearing lots of hats, depending on the growth of the business and available staff. I found President Coolidge's quote to be the important one to keep in front of me.

However, being foolishly stubborn and rigid about having your plan implemented *one* way—your way—is not what persistence is about. Referring to David Geffin again, a variety of celebrities were interviewed and asked to speak about Geffin. They repeatedly described the same asset about Geffin: "He can change on a dime." Geffin had plenty of perseverance, but when new information or opportunities came his way, he instantly made changes. Many of us resist change to our own detriment. We miss the opportunity. Being hit with problems and making changes are the challenges Geffin thrives on. Problems are not something negative. Problems are our barometers for knowing when and how to change or adjust our course, yet we must keep our eye on the overall vision of what we ultimately want and then persist again.

SETTING LIFE GOALS

Your goals don't start in the brain, they start in your heart. If you set goals from a personal perspective in the six major areas of your life, you will find your purpose will be tied into your career and all your daily activities. You can break these goals down into long-term and short-term goals, and priorities can be set by knowing your values and purpose. The six major areas are:

CAREER: What do you want to accomplish as far as your work is concerned?

FINANCIAL: *Realistically,* how much money do you want to have?

PHYSICAL: What program for physical fitness do you want to develop?

MENTAL: In what areas of your life do you wish to study and obtain more knowledge?

FAMILY: What relationships do you want to have and maintain with your family?

SPIRITUAL: What are you striving for spiritually?

Set your goals with a vision of the new and improved you. Don't get caught up in the trap of living in the past. Recognize your current reality, and then move on. It's OK to dream of good and reasonable things happening in your life. Let the dreams roll into your thoughts. Do you know people who seem to actualize their dreams often? Look at how their positive thinking works for them. A little optimism is fine, but keep your feet on the ground at the same time. It is only when dreaming takes us away from what we need to do on a daily basis that we could get into trouble, and I think most of us regularly hear, loud and clear, the constant reminders of all our basic and essential responsibilities.

Have reasonable expectations. Give yourself a frequent reality check. If you are faltering, admit it and find out why. Your present tasks and responsibilities are the most important things you have to do. There is a universal principle that states that you will not be given greater opportunities in life until you have proven that you are more capable than your present work demands. Failure to perform your present actions efficiently and successfully will delay success and may actually set in motion a situation that will cause you to go backward. Do not try to escape from the present for a better future that does not yet exist. Do what is important and eliminate or delegate the rest.

EXPAND YOUR HORIZONS ALONG WITH YOUR SOUL

Hold on to your negative thoughts and your world will unfold as those values, inner beliefs, attitudes, and perceptions become reality. Change your thoughts, and your world will unfold in new and more positive ways. In other words, if you don't change your beliefs, your life will be like this forever. Is that good news?

Fortune favors the bold. Wishful thinking will not make your dreams come true. Bold action will. He who hesitates is lost. You won't ever have to be a loser again if you take *bold action*. If you want to be free, realize that your resources are unlimited. Your mind controls your limitations or freedom from limitations, so don't let your limitations control your mind. If you think the latter, you have declared yourself a prisoner, and you will be a prisoner. Once you are fed up with that kind of thinking, you can move yourself into a kind of freedom greater than you have ever known before. You will remain where you are only as long as you wish.

You don't have to be superhuman to break through your barriers. As you may know, a certain sports shoe manufacturer's ad says, "Just do it!" As Richard Simmons once put it, "Get that paint brush in your hand and sit down with your canvas. This is your life. You are the artist and creator of your future. All you need to do is to paint the picture of your life on your imaginary canvas. Paint it the way you want it with positive brush strokes and watch it begin to unfold."

Expanding our Greater Self requires awareness, wisdom, courage, and action. The more we know, the more we realize that there is more to learn. That's the true adventure of life. You can do it with the following **ten steps to actualizing your Greater Self:**

1. Identify what is not working for you and choose to get rid of all that undermines your success. Know your current reality.

2. Get in touch with your true self, your soul, your values, your purpose, and align your true essence with your talent.

3. Clarify your vision by aligning your values and purpose with your goals. Everything you do, no matter how mundane, has meaning, a purpose.

4. Check your vision against all your personal assets. Conduct a reality check, for delusion is the enemy of the winner. Be realistic about your assets and liabilities.

5. Check your skills bank, get more information, seek advice from others, and get more training. Continuing education is vital.

6. Be self-aware and observant. Honestly check your psyche for neediness, greed, fear, jealousy, and self-righteousness. Improve your mind, with counseling if need be. Emotionally detach from all that is negative. Also, avoid being too emotionally attached to the result you want.

7. Be dynamic and innovative in *how* you create what you want. Remember, purpose is *why* you want something, goals are specifically *what* you want, and creating what you want is *how* you will accomplish getting what you want.

8. Recognize which are winning patterns and which are losing patterns. Recognize failures, correct them, and get on course—an adjusted course. An airline pilot is constantly changing the setting of his controls of the aircraft in order to remain on course to get to the final destination. If he gets word that there is an overbearing storm, he will instantly change the destination. When the red flags of warning are there, it is time to change promptly; don't stick to the original plan.

9. Set up your own rules for success and failure and know that possibility thinking will bring you what you want no matter what challenges arise. You have the power to make the impossible possible.

10. Solidify your commitment to yourself and others. Always stick to your word. Consider a win/win environment for all who are around you. You don't have to gobble up others to get what you want. As you build your own success, build your Greatest

Self along the way, for this is your most finite purpose on earth. Eleanor Roosevelt wrote, "The purpose of life, after all, is to live it, to taste experience to the utmost, to reach out eagerly and without fear for newer and richer experience."

Have you ever heard the joke about a man who kept praying every day, "Please God, please, let me win the lottery, oh please." On and on, day after day, he kept praying, and finally God said, "Hey Joe! Buy a lottery ticket!"

Eastern philosophy tends to believe that everything is predestined, and that you have little to do with making much of a difference. Western philosophy tends to be in overdrive about making things happen. Americans particularly tend to think they can control everything. To get it right, it takes a balance between these two philosophies.

We are born with our own innate capacity to create our own life dynamics. No one has the same capacity as another. Clearly we are as different as our fingerprints. No one else can make things happen for us. Not even talent agents can *make* the talent, they *discover* the talent. You can discover your own talent and then market it in your life.

Discovering our own talent (or further discovering it) involves expanding your Greater Self as opposed to your Created Self. Our gateway to expanding our sense of our Greater Self is affected by how we perceive what is *outside* us, *within* us, and *all around* us. Our ability to create is constantly affected by our sense of self, empowered and free, and it could be constantly contracted if we feel controlled and limited.

Our Created Self has been developed by all the outside stimuli that make us have a contracted sense of self. Below you will find a list of influences that affect our sense of self. They either make us contract ourselves unfavorably, or we can build them up in order to expand our Greater Self.

GATEWAYS TO EXPANDING YOUR GREATER SELF

Outside You

Sense of Safety

FROM: fear of taking risks, of rejection, of self-rejection

TO: focusing on where support can come from, and supporting yourself with positive affirmations

Sense of Self-Protection

FROM: letting others bring you down or interfere

TO: self-nurturing, allowing yourself to be nurtured, setting boundaries with others

Sense of Strength

FROM: feeling overwhelmed, controlled, weak, helpless, like a victim

TO: seeing all problems as perfect messages that you can resolve, knowing your Greater Self is your power

Within You

Sense of Compassion/Love

FROM: not loving yourself and others, feeling all used up, drained, that all you do is drudgery

TO: loving yourself, others, and loving what you do

Sense of Identity and Autonomy

FROM: the self that everyone else created for you, being jealous of others as a mask to keep you from embarking on your own endeavors

TO: recovering your self-identity, your greater self, by getting in touch with your inner self, knowing that everything that happens has a purpose

Sense of Power

FROM: giving your power away to others who criticize, control, blame, or cause chaos; having no vision

TO: following your intuition and letting it guide you fearlessly, from anger and separation to synchronicity, freedom to dream

Around You (Universal)

Sense of Possibility

FROM: resistance, impossibility, rigidity

TO: going with the flow, being receptive and creative

Sense of Connectedness

FROM: fearing to take risks, having to be perfect

TO: resourcing universal intelligence for all your needs

Sense of Abundance

FROM: sense of lack, limitation

TO: sense of unlimited resources that are attainable

Sense of Faith

FROM: disbelief, "should" or "have to" thinking, lack of belief in self

TO: knowing that universal intelligence is abundant

Remember, whatever we give our attention to, we create more of. By giving attention to your Greater Self, you will expand the capacities of your Created Self. This will allow you to handle with confidence and power any and all impossible situations you many encounter.

CHAPTER 3

Impossibility Thinking

When we perceive our lives to be on an inevitable path of continual decline, when we think that our situations are impossible and that we are failures, the likely response is to resign our lives to problems and thereby create more problems. Have you ever noticed this? People who have problems seem to create more than their share of problems. It looks like everything is happening to them or that they are very unlucky. They often appear to be victims of a cruel world where they never have a chance to succeed. In essence, they feel powerless, and this became their reality. The cycle becomes self-destructive because belief keeps creating reality and reality keeps creating belief.

LEAD WEIGHTS OF IMPOSSIBILITY

You shouldn't blame yourself when a series of things go wrong all at once. If you do, you will surely conclude that you are the victim of bad luck and therefore *you are* an unlucky person. Any of us at one time or another could be deluged by what seems to be an unending avalanche of problems. Sometimes a substantial series of problems could seem like giant ocean waves wiping us out.

Even the most mentally stable of us do reach a breaking point when too many problems and too much negativity come our way. The solution is to accept it, go with it, and then get rid of it. Instead of seeing impossible situations as happening to you, see them all as happening for a *reason*. If you hang on to misery, you create emotional, psychological, and sometimes physical lead weights that pull you down.

Changing the impossible to the possible is a matter of letting go of destructive patterns that restrict any aspect of our lives. The destructive patterns are what I call the *lead weights of impossibility*. Picture, if you will, a series of lead weights. Each one weighs five pounds and is attached to a Velcro strap. For every impossible or negative thought we have about ourselves, we are strapping on one five-pound lead weight. These lead weights prevent us from changing the impossible to the possible because we are weighed down so much that we can hardly move emotionally, psychologically, or physically. We must ask ourselves how much extra weight are we carrying around right now.

Even though we have many good qualities, our inability to succeed can be impaired by the lead weights of impossibility. Such things as doubt, guilt, anger, fear, and addictions can hold us down. As we try to move forward, we find it impossible because the weights of negativity are almost unbearable. These weights hold us down and keep us from making any real progress. They have such a stranglehold on us that changing our circumstances seems almost out of the question unless we figure out a way of releasing the lead weights of impossibility.

The mind is a marvelous thing. Through the conscious and subconscious functions, it can either assist us in creating the possible or convince us that whatever we want is impossible. The end result is determined by how we use these functions. To better understand how the mind works, in particular the subconscious, we must first understand its primary function. Although the subconscious can be used to create the possible and guide us to a successful outcome, its primary function is survival.

Through born instincts and programming, the subconscious mind sets up criteria as to what survival means to us as individuals. For each one of us it is different. Some people are concerned about survival in a relationship, some are concerned with financial survival, and for others, it is physical survival. Anything that opposes our notion of survival is challenged by the subconscious. It immediately focuses on the area of perceived danger and alerts us to take evasive action. In essence, it is always looking for perceived danger, similar to the parent who warns a child of safety hazards.

In order to protect us, the subconscious mind looks at every person, place, or situation as a potential source of danger. Another way to define danger is negativity. The mind is always looking within and without for sources of things that could go wrong and possibly hurt us emotionally, physically, or financially. It is saying, "Watch out! You know what happened last time," or "You know what? They told you this could happen."

The mind and body react, which triggers our flight or fight response. Unless we control our thinking, we continue to react in a negative way and we continue the downward spiral, which can produce anxiety, procrastination, or in some cases, severe clinical depression. The worst part is that this becomes a habitual thinking pattern. We must break out of this negative, impossibility thinker's focus, that our life is not about creating a successful, happy life but should be spent defending ourselves against all the imaginary and perceived dangers that lurk. If this is the case, then our life is only about protection, not creation or proactivity.

The bottom line is that our thoughts create our reality. If we are focused on the negative or the impossible, our subconscious will direct us to people, places, and circumstances to *prove* that we are right. In order to preserve security, the subconscious always seeks to prove that what we are thinking is in fact true.

If you think that every time you get into a relationship the person will leave you, that becomes your reality. Your subconscious then searches for people to come into your life to fulfill that perception. Whenever you are among a group of people, you will be attracted to that type of person. If you should get into a relationship with that person, he or she will eventually leave you. Then you can say, "See, I knew it. Everyone leaves me." If you think that you are going to be sick, your business will fail, or you will lose your money, your subconscious will assist you in making those assumptions a reality.

THE SPIRAL OF IMPOSSIBILITY

When life's outcomes do not match our wishes, we feel threatened. Our primary focus is on survival, so *we are no longer focused on what we want, but what we don't want.* Our motivation is based on fear, and we move away from what we don't want rather than toward what we do want. Our new goal is survival, and one of the ways we protect ourselves is to defend ourselves and our current situation. We express this by claiming that we are victims of society and other people. Our new intention is *not* to turn the impossible into the possible, but to defend ourselves and attack whatever it is we perceive to be the cause of our failure. Our energy sphere keeps contracting as we feel jealousy, blame, self-justification, anger, fear, or the need to run away. This is what causes depression. Until we are willing to change, we are stuck.

PRISON OF IMPOSSIBILITY

Every time we blame something outside of ourselves, we are in effect trying to weasel out of being accountable. Instead of being accountable, we use weasel phrases such as, "They did it to me," "I can't," "I had no choice," "I don't know what to do," "That's just the way I am," "If only . . . ," "Nobody told me that," and "If things had been different. . . ." These weasel phrases only serve to immobilize us in the present. Weasel statements are all wrapped around one basic belief which is, "I am not the cause, I am the effect." Said another way, "I am the victim."

If you believe this, you share a common trait with most prisoners. Studies of inmates in prisons show that only 3 percent of all inmates believe they are accountable for what happened to them and why they are in prison. It was their parents, poverty, lack of education, a bad influence, or drugs that caused them to end up where they are. They refuse to be accountable for the results of their own actions. When we refuse to take responsibility for where we are, we become imprisoned by our own thoughts. We are locked into the past and cannot escape into the future. The good news is that we don't have to escape this prison of impossibility; we can just walk out the front door once we take responsibility.

Freedom comes when you stop placing responsibility on others for your happiness, success, or financial condition. While this may seem harsh, no one really cares but you. In the greater scheme of things, people are more interested in their lives than they are in yours. They are too busy trying to get out of their own prison of impossibility. If you are waiting for them to help you escape, be prepared to wait for the rest of your life. This approach can only set you up for further disappointments. People can assist us, but we must take the initiative and full responsibility for where we are and where we want to be.

REDIRECTING OUR CREATIVE ENERGY

We know that we can use our mind to create the positive or the negative. Why are we so often driven toward the negative? Basically, it comes down to where we direct our creative energy. Universal energy or intelligence is like electricity running through us as creative energy. This energy is directed through the mind. The energy comes to us as positive energy. Unfortunately, we can also use the same potentially creative energy in a negative manner. This is similar to electricity. We can use electricity to turn on the lights in our homes or use it to electrocute a murderer in the electric chair. We form and mold the energy into creation through the mind. Therefore, we have the choice of creating positive energy as possible energy or negative energy as impossible energy in our lives.

Let's examine the power of creative energy within ourselves and how we can direct it. First, we must understand that our ability to use it is in direct proportion to our belief and understanding that it truly exists. Great leaders such as Christ, Gandhi, and Buddha knew how to maximize their creative energy from the universal substance and translate it into positive manifestation or results. The basis of all their teachings is that you also have that same creative energy in you. The manner in which you use it determines the results you will experience in your life. Let's look at some examples. In its simplest manifestation, it can be experienced when you walk into a room with people in it. Have you ever noticed a heaviness or troublesome atmosphere, even though no one has said anything or acted out of the ordinary? You just get that feeling. This is an *energy field.*

The energy field around us changes as we change emotionally, spiritually, and psychologically. The reverse is also true. Our psychological and physical states are affected by the energy fields around us. Think of the universe as one dynamic energy field that sustains us. If we think negatively of ourselves, we disconnect from that source of energy. In order to overcome the impossible, you must have a sense that you are bigger than any problem you face. The *you* I am referring to is not the Created Self you think you ought to be, but your Greater Self. A simple but profound way to think about this energy is to think that you are at the center of a large sphere or ball of energy that expands and contracts like a balloon. When you are negative, upset, angry, or scared, this energy balloon contracts. This limits your power to change. Alternately, when you are confident, joyful, and compassionate, the energy sphere expands. All the solutions for possibility are open to you. You even look and feel different, not just to yourself, but to others.

All problems in life can be viewed in the context of this contraction or expansion phenomenon. We have been conditioned to deal with life's problems by contracting our power or energy. The process of contraction and depression continues until with each contraction, all opportunity literally disappears from our lives. This is the true definition of depression. We have the ability to repattern our way of thinking. To do this, we must learn to relax, trust, and let go. Then our energy field is free to expand.

CIRCLE OF POSSIBILITY

We tend to take the path of least resistance. Resistance to change is in direct proportion to our comfort zone. We will call this our *circle of possibility*. Our circle of possibility is created by the thoughts we have been thinking and the things we have done. Anything new that we have not done or thought before makes us feel uncomfortable. Uncomfortable thoughts or the prospect of doing something we have not done before increases our anxiety level. This in turn makes us feel even more uncomfortable and causes us to believe that what we want to do is impossible. This discouragement, which comes from believing what we want is impossible, often causes us to give up even before we start. When we move past our comfort level, we find the adventure, excitement, and satisfaction we desire.

Have you ever said to yourself, "I don't want to do that because it makes me uncomfortable"? You're not alone. This is a normal response when most people are confronted with a new situation. Unfortunately, most people use discomfort as a reason or excuse for not doing something. To illustrate this, picture a circle around you.

Circle of Possibility

You are in the middle of the circle. The circle represents your circle of possibility. Everything outside the circle represents things that you have not experienced . . . things that make you uncomfortable. This also is your circle of protection. Just slightly outside your circle are your goals or even problems that come into your life. When faced with new challenges, opportunities, or obstacles, they begin to intrude upon your circle. The tendency is to rush to the outer limits of your circle and set up defenses. In some cases, you'll pretend that whatever is outside your circle isn't there. The problem is, the very thing you want is usually outside your circle. It keeps banging up against your circle until it gets your attention. You can either try to avoid it, pretend it is not there, or make a decision to resolve it or achieve it.

Your desire to achieve it or resolve it prompts you to go the edge of the circle and break through. The only way you can get to it is to break through your circle just enough to bring it within your circle of possibility. Once it is within your circle, you can deal with it. Now an interesting thing happens. Each thing you bring inside your circle of possibility expands your comfort zone. In other words, the circle becomes larger and extends beyond your ability to deal with the situation. Now that situation that used to be beyond your limits is within your reach. Not only are you able to deal with it, but you can expand your circle.

The degree to which we are happy or not happy is in direct proportion to how much control your circle of possibility has over you. If it has more control over you than you do of yourself, then you experience unhappiness, anxiety, and depression. There are four factors that cause us to stay within our circle of impossibility: fear, guilt, unworthiness, and anger. Let's look at some examples of the lead weights of impossibility and how they make change seem nearly impossible.

Fear

We stay within our limited circle of possibility because of fear. We often feel fear even when we are just skeptical, fearing disappointment. Fear is the mind-talk that prevents you from hearing your intuition. It is probably the most common limiting emotion. The basis of fear is the flight or fight syndrome. Remember, our mind is always trying to protect us. Survival, not success and happiness, are the primary goals. We fear what we don't know, and that fear keeps us from taking action. Not taking action keeps us ignorant, and ignorance creates more fear. Thus the cycle repeats itself.

Any time we venture into the unknown, we will have fears. Everyone has fears. For some of us it's death, public speaking, loss of love, animals, darkness, flying, or fear of losing at the races. After working with thousands of people, it has become clear to me that we create our fears as well as our dreams, and they happen just as we planned them to.

In a recent interview with pop singer Gloria Estefan after her near-fatal accident that involved a severe spinal injury, she said that all her life she had a fear that she would be crippled in an accident. She said, "I was afraid I would be crippled and not be able to walk, and I have been afraid of that my entire life. When the accident happened, I thought, it's finally here." Another lady got what she didn't really wish for when she kept complaining about having to pay for her auto insurance for so many years, and yet she never had a claim. In the next week, she got her claim. They say, "Watch what you wish for; it might come true!"

Many people have a fear of making mistakes. A major lead weight is our bundle of past mistakes. We all have made mistakes, but we insist on playing them over and over in our head instead of letting them go and moving on. Perhaps you have gained weight, lost your job, ruined your health, or had a relationship that was self-destructive. Because of these mistakes, you have convinced yourself that you can never be in shape again, never find another good job, never restore your health, or never find someone to love you.

In the process of expanding our circle of possibility, we are going to make mistakes. There is no way to avoid them. However, mistakes should not be construed as total and irreversible failures. Mistakes are just behaviors or methods that do not work. It is important to provide a buffer zone in your circle where you allow yourself and others an opportunity to make mistakes without judgment. This will allow you to look at mistakes and self-correct rather than wasting valuable energy on what should have happened or what you should have done. Consider all mistakes as feedback, not failures. Instead, keep the lesson and throw away the experience.

One of the biggest fears is the fear of failure. However, there is really no way you can fail in life. Failure is a relative term and a value judgment. What looks like failure to you may not be failure to someone else. If you don't earn $50,000 a year, you may consider yourself a failure. However, someone else may feel that if they earn $10,000 a year, they are a success. Failure is determined by the rules we set up in life concerning success and failure. All we have to do is change the rules. More importantly, we must not let others make the rules for us.

Recently, I read a list of famous and successful individuals that had been fired from a job at least once. One of them was the talk show host, Sally Jessy Raphael. She was fired by approximately twenty radio and television stations before she finally found success with her television talk show. She certainly never gave up. Thomas Edison made 5,000 mistakes before he discovered the light bulb. So just think, if he gave up at the 4,999th try, who knows how long we would have had to wait for someone else to discover the light bulb! Do you think Thomas Edison feared failure? I tell people, "If you are not making at least ten mistakes a day, you're doing something wrong."

How to Be More Fearless

There are those who say we can get rid of our fears. Perhaps that is so. However, I believe that life without fear is not an option that is available to us. I prefer to approach it from this manner: Instead of *fighting* our fears or trying to get *rid* of them, we can *neutralize* their power over us by just *accepting* them and then taking immediate *action*. As simple as it may seem, the only difference between successful people and those who are not successful is their response to fear. Let's face it, we are all afraid. Successful people are afraid, but they take *action;* they don't get immobilized by their fears.

Overcoming fear requires that we plunge into the very thing that makes us afraid so that, in the end, our fear will be eliminated. Think of tackling your fear as a means of conquest, building spiritual and emotional muscle. As you start each day, contemplate your daily plan and envision yourself going through it, especially when you will be taking on new challenges that worry or frighten you. If you are in balance, with the mind, body, and spirit connected, you can overcome your fears about what threatens you.

If your biggest fear is that you will be a failure, I have good news for you. You can never really fail, because you can never fail as a *person*. Your job can fail, your finances can fail, your business can fail, your relationship can fail, but that's not you. All those things are outside of you. They can all be changed or corrected. The problem comes when you start believing that you are what you have and what you do. The solution to overcoming the fear of failure is to recognize that you cannot fail as a person. The key is to separate yourself from what you have and what you do.

Guilt—The Gift That Keeps on Giving

It is critical to recognize the insidious nature of this emotion in that it can have such crippling, long-term consequences. In adulthood, the guilt-prone person can suffer from underlying, free-flowing guilty feelings even when nothing logical supports their presence. Feelings of guilt can manifest in people's dreams along with guilt's twin, anxiety. This may be one of the first and foremost components of an unworkable moral code to erase if a person wants to achieve complete health. Such crippling emotions and mental patterns only get in the way of personal growth. They really lend nothing to our quest to remove impossible constraints and open the way for possible fulfillment.

When we think or act in a manner that produces guilty feelings, our responses to guilt are to promise not to do it again and/or to punish ourselves by feeling bad. We rationalize that when good people do bad things, they are supposed to feel bad. Feeling bad is the price we must pay for violating our beliefs about what good people do. In every area of our lives we have beliefs about how good people should think and behave. When we act that way, it proves that we are a good person. When we fall short of the ideal image, our unquestioned reaction may be to feel guilty and anxious.

As a child, you were given a standard of perfection to live up to by your parents, religious teachers, and other role models. As you moved into adolescence, you started adding your own set of beliefs about perfection based on input from your family, friends, peer groups, and the effects of advertising and other well-intentioned sources. As an adult, you try to live according to that model of good and bad, based on those beliefs.

Unfortunately, we rarely question our beliefs about good and bad. If our beliefs came from authority figures such as our parents, teachers, or religion, we just assume that what they told us is true. Whether they are true or not is not the issue. More importantly, how do these programmed images produce feelings of guilt in our daily lives that then affect our self-worth? The important point here is that we must distinguish between when we should change our actions and when we should change our beliefs about our actions. If our actions are producing a negative result, the easiest way to change our actions is to change our beliefs first.

We must determine the validity of our beliefs by asking ourselves questions. Where did I get this belief? Who told me it was true? Did someone tell me in order to control me? Did they really know what they were talking about, or are they just passing their programmed beliefs on to me for my own good?

Instead of feeling bad, we can use guilt constructively by changing our belief so that our energy is not directed toward feeling bad every time we do something or don't do something that others have told us is bad or wrong. The key here is to understand that good people sometimes do bad things. Bad things can be defined as things that produce a negative result. We must separate the doer (us) from the end result (action). In other words, your actions may sometimes be bad or inappropriate, but you are not a bad person—or a good person for that matter. You are just you, doing good or bad things that produce positive or negative results.

Keep in mind that your Greater Self is neither good nor bad, because at the spiritual level there is no judgment. However, your Created Self is only human and still has imperfections built on false beliefs.

The most formidable guilt-producing statement you can make is, "I could have done better." That is entirely false. To *know* better is not sufficient to *do* better. Knowledge is unrelated to action and is intrinsically an intellectual process. We know we should not smoke, use drugs, overeat, and hurt ourselves or others, but we do these things anyway. The only way this will change is when we come to the point where we realize the pain of our actions is greater than the price we will have to pay to change them. At that point, we will stop doing negative things to ourselves and to others. Guilt only serves to make us feel bad about our thoughts and actions, and it is a poor replacement for consciously choosing to rid ourselves of undesirable ways of running our lives.

So, when you do things that you feel guilty about, just say to yourself, "Obviously, I have not reached the point where I am perfect. I am only human and I am still learning. I am not going to feel bad, but I am going to use this opportunity to remind myself to do better the next time." If the pain of your actions is great enough, you will not do it again. If you got away with it this time and did not pay the full price for your actions, you will probably do it again. Just keep reminding yourself that the price is getting too high and now might be a good time to change your thinking more quickly so that you take better action in the future, without requiring pain to compel you.

If guilt is feeling discouraged, feeling punished, and self-punishing, then we can replace it by being productive, reliable, sincere, cooperative, lucky, involved, tender, gentle, and purposeful. Learn to replace stationary and backsliding guilt with positive forward motion. The more you truly become a friend to yourself, recognize your life's purpose, and engage the Greater Self in your daily dealings, the more you will sense that guilt is relaxing its hold in your mental makeup.

Action will increasingly replace stagnant self-flagellation. Guilt can be a convenient replacement for taking effective action and accepting responsibility. It's as though we childishly believe that appropriate suffering releases us from capable, adult behavior. As such, guilt becomes a thinly masked form of selfishness. Guilt is a poor substitute for engaging fully in life. As nothing more than self-blame, it is one of the more fruitless, circular nonsolutions in which we invest valuable energy.

Allow yourself to release the hold guilt has on you and move on to more effective, self-loving means of changing your behavior. Hair shirts are out . . . constructive thoughts and concrete action are in.

Unworthiness

Self-worth comes from the Greater Self. If you know your true nature, you will better recognize and understand the true nature of those around you. The more you realize about yourself, the better you will understand yourself and others.

Don't be afraid to let others see a weakness in you. Some people are so horrified at the thought that someone would discover a weakness in them that they will even lie and manipulate in order to cover for themselves. Some people will take this so far that they will even let others suffer consequences for them.

A televised report on human behavior set up the following situation and played it out. A job applicant was put in a waiting room that contained a table with several party platters of food. The applicant was told not to take any, as the trays were for a celebration to be held later on. A hidden camera showed the woman gave in to her temptation by eating a variety of items. When the prospective employee was asked if she took any of the food, she said no. She was asked again because the interviewer stated that they noticed that some of the food was missing. Another employee was brought into the room. This man had stopped in earlier when the applicant was alone in the room. The employee was asked in front of the applicant if he saw her take any of the food. Even though he said he had not, the applicant, when asked, stated that the employee took the food and not herself.

I have also seen executives lie over matters that were not so important, yet they were willing to hurt another on the job, all because the executives just could not bear for anyone to know they made any kind of error. It certainly is not very honest when people are so preoccupied with covering up their mistakes that they will even manipulate others in order to be right.

Is your self-worth so fragile and on such a thin foundation that you fear being wrong? Do you have a problem with saying, "Oops, I made a mistake. Sorry"? I hope not. When we try to cover up our flaws, along with the cover-up, we block any chance of demonstrating our undiscovered, innate strengths.

Twelve Surefire Ways to Destroy Your Self-Worth

1. Have a lack of faith in yourself and whatever you believe in.

2. Complain, criticize, blame, bring others down, and nitpick. Divide people and be disruptive. Constantly compare and measure yourself up—really up—above others. Hold others down so they won't get ahead of you.

3. Don't be flexible, be a quitter, and be satisfied with less.

4. Associate with weak people. Work along with people who are going nowhere. Worse yet, let them make up your mind for you.

5. Be a know-it-all, a nerd.

6. Be a taker.

7. Use this kind of weak language: "Impossible, tired, problems, unreal, what's in it for me." Frown a lot and don't attend a self-improvement program.

8. Talk about all the things that are wrong with people. Talk too much, and wait for things to happen . . . nothing will.

9. Take a job with no chance for advancement. Split at five o'clock. Do no more. Do only what benefits yourself, and your limited perspective will only allow you to see uninteresting short-term benefits. Then you will not be able to see the long-term benefits that may be of help to you in the long run.

10. Deliberately scatter yourself, spread yourself too thin.

11. Satisfy your lack of self-worth by being a workaholic. This is another way to only think of yourself.

12. Dwell on things not working out, and imagine that they could only get worse.

What You Can Do to Build Your Self-Worth

If we don't feel we are worthy, competent, or deserving, every time we try to embrace the possible, our subconscious says, "Remember, you told me that you are a jerk, no one will ever love you, you can't do anything right, and you're not good enough. Who do you think you are? We know that I am a powerless victim. Don't even try." Then we say, "There is no way I can be, do, or have this." Your subconscious replies, "Now you are being realistic." Then, when we don't get what we want, we say, "See, I knew it would not work out. I was right all along."

This inner dialogue is more predominant than we think. Many people try to cover it up by appearing confident. Some go to the extreme, bordering on arrogance. In reality, they are merely involved in an attempt to hide the fact that they feel incompetent and unworthy.

Where did all this come from? How did we get this way? Without getting into the usual psychobabble about how most of it came from our childhood, suffice to say that we were not born this way. Our well-intentioned parents tried to bring us up to do the right thing. Unfortunately, by tradition, they determined that the best way to do this was to get us to focus on what we were doing wrong. "Don't do this. You can't do that. You're bad. How could you think like that?" The problem with parenting is that, even though we are well-intentioned, parenting is really about passing insanity from one generation to the next. This is because your parents were probably brought up in the same way. Most of us do not examine our beliefs to determine if they are valid or workable. Instead, we just accept that what we believe is true and spend our lives trying to convince ourselves, our children, and others that these beliefs are indeed true. The problem that arises is that we have false beliefs and are operating under certain value assumptions.

It all starts from our infancy, when our parents mostly warned us of dangers like, "Don't touch that electrical outlet," and "Don't touch that hot iron." Most parents are busy and in a rush, so most of their time communicating with their children involves a bunch of "don't do that" messages intended for their basic human need for safety and survival. Ideally, parents would spend *most* of their time, no matter how busy they are, building up their children's psyches with positive messages that reinforce what their children are doing right, not wrong. Further, they would even encourage their young to do new things well. They would show them how to try to do new things and take risks, but they would not criticize their mistakes as they try.

Unfortunately, our early years were likely spent going through a conditioning process that told us that we were basically bad, stupid, incompetent, and sinners. The only way we thought we could prove otherwise and ever hope to get a little appreciation or approval in this life was to do what others wanted, all the while thinking, "In this way I can earn my worthiness." We reinforce a pattern that positive or possible thoughts about ourselves would be good, but negative or impossible thoughts are more realistic and comfortable. Every time we have possibility thoughts, we automatically check them against this primary belief that we are not worthy or competent, and the answer comes up, "Error!" Negative or impossible thoughts feel customary and therefore normal, comfortable, and believable.

One thing you can do to build your self-worth is stop letting just anybody who comes along cut you down. Say no to criticism. If you did not ask for feedback, then it is not welcome, and even if you did ask for some feedback, someone else's critical delivery style is still unacceptable. Someone could say to you, "I liked your report, but I have one criticism." Here you are, wide open for a shot or ready to duck, and your critic could be totally off base, yet what they proceeded to tell you will play on your mind for a long time. Who needs this?

On the other hand, it must be said that giving criticism when you were not asked to do so should be avoided. The best way to tell someone about something they are doing that concerns you is to tell them that it makes *you feel bad* when they do whatever action it is that directly involves you. If someone has a drinking problem, you could say, "It makes me feel frightened to watch you walk out the door that way. I am afraid you will hurt yourself." (Of course, we have heard enough public service announcements to know that we had better do all we can to stop a drunk driver.)

You can't expect people to change their general habits and behaviors because of your advice. Although your feelings are probably not going to compel them to change, *you* will feel much better by having a chance to release your feelings. This is the purpose in expressing your feelings and concerns to another, because you care and you are filled with feelings of worry, concern, or annoyance. If the person eventually takes heed of what you say, great.

When people try to criticize you, you can attempt to coach them on the manner in which they can approach you with their concern; otherwise, say no to criticism. If you want feedback about something you are questioning about yourself, then ask someone whose views you respect. However, you do not have to believe the answer. It's still your life, and your experiences, and you can only *consider* someone else's thoughts as you must make your own decisions.

Finally, if you feel too much anger toward some people, tell them you have got to go sort things out, or do some soul searching. Some people are safe to be around, and some people are not. The ones who understand these kinds of boundaries and ground rules during conflict are the people that it is safe to work things through with. There are an abundance of communication skills and conflict resolution workshops and books that can detail these—and many more—important communication techniques. Since relationships appear to be the most challenging thing we face in life, continuing to advance our interpersonal skills would make our lives ten times better, and we won't be as easily disturbed or angered.

Unworthiness can leave us feeling unloved, deserted, melancholy, filled with despair, unimportant, unacceptable, and uncared for. It's OK to take a look at what seems to give you the blues, but only get into it enough to realize what elements affected your getting the blues. One surefire way to perpetuate feelings of unworthiness is to carry out feeling sorry for yourself to the point of becoming a victim.

We can turn around any feelings of unworthiness by doing some soul-searching, self-evaluation, and some self-improvement that ultimately builds our feeling of worthiness. Some of the qualities that we want to achieve to lift us out of unworthiness are excitement, feeling alive, delight, trust, tenderness, being congruent, perception, balance, and feeling at one with people. If we could have more faith in the people around us, and if we could have more faith in ourselves, the world would be a better place. As Sam Ervin, Jr., said, "Have faith!— Faith lets us walk in those areas outside the boundaries of human thought." So don't give up your belief in the goodness of others and your belief in yourself. Most of all, be loyal and true to yourself, not in a selfish way, in the right way.

Anger

Have you noticed that the word *anger* is one letter short of *danger?* Anger always seems to be directed *at* something: at things, at others, and at ourselves. It is about how we measure up, or actually, how we or others *don't* measure up.

All unhappiness is caused by *comparison.* Seeing life as a *competition* against others or even a competition against your own expectations brings about great frustration, resulting in anger. We are conditioned to see competition as a way of life. It's all around us in sports, business, keeping up with the Joneses, between family members and siblings, and in advertising. In this age of the information highway, we are constantly exposed to high competition as a means of survival. We become conditioned into believing that beating others makes the battle worthwhile. However, this competitiveness has no deeper purpose; it is meaningless. Is a painful battle worth the end, especially when you could achieve the same end without bloodshed? Certainly not, when there is no reason to hurt others in order to gain what you want.

After seeing a high school coach hammer out bombastic and degrading screams at his students, including telling them belittling statements such as that they were worthless, I found it hard to believe that if the parents of these kids knew or understand the repercussions of what he was yelling, they would not have found this particular football team a worthwhile training program for their sons. Such intensely negative remarks are not what motivates a football team. Yeah, yell and shout, but make it a lot of positive yelling like, "You can do it!" The coach should reinforce what skills they do best, pointing out their team's winning qualities. This is the way to motivate a team. The coach could even get his boys believing *they* themselves are the fierce warriors, not the coach. His being a degrading brute and telling them they are worthless is what was actually worthless.

If beating others down to nothing is what winning is about, I'll pass. Only losers need to win, if they can't be happy unless they defeat others. If you think this is the way to go, then others will have control over your fulfillment, and every time things do not work out, you're going to be real mad at yourself and others. Competition can be fun, but only as long as it is not at the expense of the livelihood of others. Thinking we must win at all costs psychologically enslaves us. If instead you achieve a victory without having to relive it and relish it, seeing it over and over in your mind, then your true self will be free of depending on the achievement. So just achieve, be glad, and move on.

If competition is not what makes you angry, then it is usually an extension of it, such as when you believe your survival has been threatened by someone. No matter what, the anger we feel is *always* about our relationship to everything. It involves the way we relate to everyone, including ourselves, and everything, such as our job and our possessions.

Anger manifests itself in us in a variety of forms, such as rage (explosive), implosive anger, and passive aggression (which is anger taken out subtly but deviously on others). Knowing the ways anger manifests itself in us gives us ways to get rid of it. Often, we try to *escape* from it instead of facing it and resolving it. Ultimately, we would want to know how to get rid of it once and for all.

Ways We Try to Escape Anger

We have different ways to avoid anger, one being to run away from it, seeking an escape for protection. Another way we try to escape anger is to attempt to control the situation by trying not to feel anything, by taking it all up into our heads. You'll often hear people say, "You're overanalyzing the situation." When we do this, we do not have a full and clear picture of the situation and all of its repercussions on others.

Then there is the old silent treatment. A study of marital relationships found one behavior pattern that made it nearly impossible to work things out, and this is the person who withdraws from his or her spouse. These people refuse to talk to their spouse about a problem, even later on. When someone shuts down like this, that person will soon find that the spouse will leave, since there is no one to work it out or argue it out with. The person who becomes so automatically conditioned to freeze up when things get tough really needs to learn how to do some emotional release work and learn how to express, even with some anger, what he or she really feels. What these people need to know is that it is safer to duke it out (with a reasonable partner), than to lose such a valuable partner. If they shut down all the time in each relationship, they will just lose one partner after another. They should realize that problems always can be resolved one way or another, rather than refusing discussion and therefore making their relationship impossible. The overly quiet type of people, manifested in their worst form, could suddenly become dangerous when they finally explode or act out in some way. Whenever we hear of a serial killer, we hear that the person was very quiet and withdrawn. Now, *that's* what is dangerous. It is safer to appropriately express anger than to withhold it.

Many people manifest the instinctive escape processes mentioned above by using religion or spirituality to try to pray away their anger. Religion and spirituality are about building a close relationship to God, or whatever you believe is your higher power, but that source cannot eliminate human feeling. It can help us work through the feelings, but they have to be felt and dealt with. Your emotions are in your body, and you need to take care of them. All the meditating in the world is not going to truly release anger. It may temporarily help you calm yourself down, but as soon as you go back to your routine, the lingering problem is still bristling. The problem must have a resolution. Only in some situations, where there is nothing you can do, acceptance is needed, and then perhaps some meditating or praying can soothe any wounds. If there is something you can do or must do to solve a problem, face it and do it. Otherwise, the silent treatment is sure to make you fail.

Finally, some people try to escape their problems and anger with addictions to alcohol, drugs, sex, dependency on others . . . you know the list. Any of these methods used to attempt to escape from problems and anger will not make your fears and frustrations go away. Anger builds up over a lifetime unless you do something to release your pent-up anger.

Enlist Some Techniques That Release Anger

Wherever our angers come from—childhood, a past job, or current situations—they build up and they must be released. The way to get rid of the buildup is to use some techniques for reviewing your history and patterns of anger and get them out on the table with a counselor, your spouse, or anyone who is very close to you. You might need to use some deprogramming techniques that replace the old angers with new positive thoughts such as affirmations. We've had a lot of years of negativity conditioning us to see mostly the impossible. The fast track for deprogramming all that built-up stuff would be to make your own affirmation tape where you calmly make positive statements about yourself, your knowledge, your skills, and your talents. Some suggest that you state each one three times. Change those old tapes playing in your head to a new tape, and have a new lease on life.

Other methods for getting rid of anger include all sorts of physical activities like walking, dancing, hiking, pounding pillows, and screaming (while you are alone in your car or out in the wilderness). This stuff works. Exercise works well. I have noticed a feeling of exhilaration whenever I exercise (and I haven't even gone so far as getting to the stage of what they call "the jogger's high"). Isn't it great to consider that a way for you to expand your circle of possibility is by simply doing some of the *physical* activities mentioned? Try it. Remember, people who *fly* into a rage always make a *bad* landing, and you can avoid this by flying in some better directions . . . like to the athletic club.

Humor—Your Most Powerful Ally

One of the most powerful tools we can use to break through the barriers of impossibility is humor. Although I am a serious person, I try to see the humorous side of most situations. In fact, some people are taken by surprise when I make a joke about things that are supposed to be serious. Those who know me well have said that, when it comes to humor, "Everything is fair game with you. Nothing is sacred." It's true. I often use humor as a means of defusing a situation either by shock value or just by trying to put things into perspective.

I remember one time I was flying into Buffalo. As the plane was landing, the wheels crashed through the concrete runway. Apparently there was a weak spot or a washout under the runway and it couldn't hold the weight of the plane. Anyway, the wheels went through the runway and literally snapped off. The plane landed on its belly and we went scraping across the concrete. Sparks were flying everywhere and the sound of metal against concrete was incredible. After we stopped, the pilot said we were OK and there was no fire, but we would have to evacuate the plane immediately by sliding down the emergency chute.

Everyone was panicked. People were screaming and crying, but no one was hurt. I don't know why, but at that moment I thought to myself, *Gee, what is everyone worried about? We're all alive.* My next statement shocked a couple of passengers because I said jokingly as I was getting ready to jump down the chute, "That's great, now how are we going to get the luggage out of here?"

Sure, it was a serious situation, but I used humor to help defuse the seriousness of the situation and to put things into perspective. My message was, "We are alive, so why worry; except, of course, about our luggage." Throughout this book we are going to discuss some serious issues. I just wanted to warn you that often I will try to put things into perspective through the use of humor or looking at things on the light side. So, make it a fun journey. I don't have all the answers for you. But work with me, and we will come up with some answers that will be highly beneficial. Most of all, let's try to learn more about ourselves and have fun in the process.

If the following behaviors are indicative of our anger: hostility, hatred, resentment, antagonism, sarcasm, withholding, rejecting, fiery, overwrought, incensed, and put upon; then the following opposite behaviors can free us from it: acceptance, willingness, interest, receptiveness, invigoration, encouragement, appreciation, being tuned in, being deserving, openness, worthiness, optimism, approachability, understandingness, and forgiveness. Now we know what the goal is. Turn your anger into enthusiasm.

As Dale Carnegie said, "Enthusiasm makes the difference!—The way to acquire enthusiasm is to believe in what you are doing and in yourself and to want to get something definite accomplished. . . . Enthusiasm will follow . . . as night the day."

CHANGING IMPOSSIBILITY
THINKING TO POSSIBILITY
THINKING

It is obivious that impossibility thinking severely limits our lives. All the problems you face in life are caused by your perception, how you *see* what happens to you and what you perceive to be real about your ability to face problems. This perception has formed a Created Self that includes personality traits that are both positive and negative. If you want to change any situation from the impossible to the possible, you must first change your perception of who you are rather than what you tend to believe you do or have. Where you are and what you have is the result or sum total of how you perceive your Created Self instead of allowing the real you, your Greater Self, to command your own success. This can be done by changing impossibility thinking into possibility thinking.

CHAPTER 4

Possibility Thinking

Success, happiness, and good luck are available to any of us who are ready for it. Unfortunately, most of us do not know how to unlock the door. We sit in mental prisons and wait for our life to change, never realizing that the door to the prison is open—there are no guards. You may not be aware of it, but your attitude is either the *key* or the *lock* on the door to fulfillment.

POSITIVE THINKING VS. POSSIBILITY THINKING

Thus far, we have considered how impossibility thinking keeps us from having what we truly want in life. The obvious answer would seem to be to just think positively and believe that what we want is possible. On the surface, this seems reasonable, but in the real world, it is not entirely true. As an example, look at something near you right now. Focus on it. Now think positively to yourself that what you are looking at will move. Now, mentally command it to move. Keep thinking positively. What happened? I think you get the idea.

Although there may have been a few avatars in India or elsewhere in the world who might have done this, this is not a basic human capability. Most of us haven't reached that level of awareness yet. The mind is powerful, but not powerful enough to *will* things to happen. The problem with positive thinking is that there is a gap between our current reality and what we want to happen. This gap, if not understood and handled properly, can create anxiety, confusion, and even mental illness.

THE POWER OF POSITIVE FOCUS

There is a big difference between *focusing* on the positive and thinking positively. When we are focusing on the positive, we are not saying that things are different than our reality. We are not in denial. What our focus does is make us aware of the possibilities. It gives us direction. Whatever we focus on, we create more of. In every situation we have a choice. We can focus on the positive or the negative. If you look at what is wrong with you and/or the world, that is exactly what you will see. Since you cannot look in two directions at once, you will miss the possible. On the other hand if you focus on the possible, you not only tend to feel better, but you will see new possibilities that you had not seen before. Think back to the object you were trying to move with positive thinking. If you focus on the positive, instead of thinking positively you will say to yourself, "That object will not move. That is the reality. But I have the ability to move it if I choose. I think I will get up and do something about it."

The difference between the positive thinker and the possibility thinker is that the positive thinker says, "I am happy," when he is not, "I am rich," when he is poor, "I am healthy," when he is sick. The possibility thinker says, "I am unhappy now, but if I do this I can be happy," "I don't have any money right now, but if I focus on this possible opportunity, I can turn it around," "I am sick right now, but if I do this, I can be well." The difference between positive thinking and possibility thinking is that the possibility thinker does not deny reality. One of the best and most amusing analogies I have ever heard about a positive thinker is the man who fell from the top floor of a fifteen story building, and on the way down you could hear him screaming, "So far, so good!"

CAN YOU HAVE ANYTHING YOU WANT?

Is anything possible, or are there limitations? Turn on any talk show, read any self-help book, and we are told by the experts that the causative factor behind all of our psychological and emotional ills is low self-esteem. The cure, of course, is high self-esteem. The continuous message is that if one has high self-esteem, one is healthy and can achieve a healthy outcome in relationships, business, health, and finances. In many respects, this is absolutely true, but there is also a pathological downside, which can be termed, *misguided high self-esteem*. Misguided high self-esteem can often increase our persistence on fruitless endeavors.

The illusion of invulnerability is often the cause of impossible situations. This overconfidence comes about from the belief that somehow, through positive thinking and good intentions, we can avoid the negative things that happen to us and to other people. We overestimate our prospects of success or survival by misperceiving our current situation.

Contrary to the claims of positive thinkers who claim you can have anything you want, realistically there are certain limitations. First, there are physical limitations. If you are in Florida, you can't be in California at the same time. There are financial limitations. If you want to buy a new car and don't have any money, all the positive thinking in the world will not help you. For a clearer definition of what is possible, let's say that if someone else can, or has, achieved it, it is possible for you. Second, if it is available for you to achieve, you can have it. Setting a reasonable goal that is measurable in time makes the difference.

GOOD INTENTIONS, INEFFECTIVE APPROACH

Many impossible situations are created as a result of the attainment of normal, healthy goals. The reason for this is that we chronically employ ineffective approaches and fail to change or correct our ineffective behavior, especially when we recognize that what we are doing is not working. One of the most commonly ineffective approaches is overpersistence while using ineffective behavior. Many people will persist at something beyond all reason. They need to prove something to themselves, or they don't want to be wrong or make a mistake. In order to avoid this, they keep pressing on with ineffective behavior patterns that eventually lead them to an impossible situation. Often, we observe this in the relationships of others where we can see the results of someone's stubborn persistence.

Many people are guided by well-intentioned motives but experience setbacks, problems, misfortunes, and other difficulties because of ineffective approaches. Most of the time it involves misjudgment. They misjudge themselves and their circumstances. These errors in judgment lead to setting themselves up in impossible situations. They may not see what is possible and probable. Instead, they overestimate what they are capable of achieving at the present time. An important point here is that when we have brought failure and suffering into our lives, although it was never our goal, many times it is a by-product of our effort to obtain a desirable goal.

Overpersistence in the wrong direction will not get you what you want or take you where you want to go. It only creates more impossible situations. Persistence has always been touted as a virtue, which it can be if we are headed in the right direction, but excessive and pathological persistence in the wrong direction can only lead us to the depths of impossibility. Most self-help literature illustrates the virtue of persistence by pointing out those who have perceived and eventually triumphed, despite impossible situations. They point out that those who give up too easily are nothing more than quitters. While persistence may be a virtue in some cases, it can also be destructive. Some approaches or strategies simply are ineffective, and through persistence we multiply the number of failures that we experience, which often leads to disaster.

As an example, the investor who buys a certain stock and then sees that it continues to drop, won't bail out, even though he will clearly lose even more money. Instead of having a stop loss, he hangs on. Another instance would be a person who remains in a relationship that is self-destructive, where the partner does not want to communicate for resolution or get help. The person stays in the relationship because he or she is more concerned with *persevering* or *saving* the relationship than having a healthy lifestyle. Saving the relationship becomes paramount, rather than saving the individuals in the relationship. Take the student who pursues a career path, only to find out that it is not right for him, yet he keeps on the path because he does not want to be a quitter. The point here is that it is important to know when to quit. Quitting is not always bad. We must learn to make an accurate assessment regarding when persistence is necessary and when it is self-destructive, and then make a healthy adjustment in those negative behaviors that keep us on the wrong track. People find all kinds of ways of behaving in opposition to what they really want. Many of these behavior patterns are deliberate and intentional. However, this doesn't mean that we are self-destructive or intend a destructive consequence. On one hand, some people deliberately take actions that will clearly and definitely bring harm to themselves, while others do not foresee the consequences of their actions. They do not want to fail or sabotage their relationships, health, careers, or finances, yet they act in ways that destroy their own efforts to reach a positive outcome.

Other people fall in the middle somewhere. They can see the possibility of harm but ignore it or downplay it. When they look back, they recognize that the outcome was, in many cases, foreseeable and avoidable. This may include wearing a seat belt, using a condom, not smoking, compulsive gambling, alcohol consumption, or substance abuse. At the time, they ignore the risks and focus on the immediate pleasure.

A significant portion of impossible situations are created in our lives when we take unnecessary risks. We may not be seeking self-harm or self-destruction, in fact we try to avoid it, but the real risk is our own behavior, which seems to turn against us when our problems intensify. Things might have turned out well, but they didn't. Not everyone who smokes will have lung cancer, or who is in an accident without a seat belt will get hurt, or who has sex without a condom will get AIDS. Nonetheless, the risks are there and the facts were well known in advance.

YOUR DOMINANT THOUGHT
CREATES YOUR DESTINY

We are certain, based on quantum biology (which is the application of quantum physics to biology), that our neurology is driven by our dominant thoughts. Our beliefs, whether they are true or false, structure us in a way that shapes the very anatomy and physiology of our nervous system. Besides the importance of our nervous system on our physical movement, the nervous system, particularly our brain, keeps reinforcing what we believe to be true, whether it is true or not. In essence, we live our life conditioned by a programmed reality that may cause us to get off course and end up where we don't want to be. This can lead to a feeling of helplessness, victimization, depression, or even despair.

We often experience these feelings and emotions after a series of setbacks or defeats, such as failed romance, losing our business or job, or loss of money. We decide to give up and start to believe that there are forces beyond our control that make directing our own lives impossible. This can be a particularly destructive pattern because even when conditions become favorable for success, we do not see the opportunity. Instead, we stay stuck in impossible situations or, what's worse, we continue to set ourselves up for failure.

This behavior pattern is predominant in minority groups that have been oppressed in our society. The cycle of discrimination, failure, helplessness, and apathy tend to make many minorities think that the American dream is not available to them, but only available to the white or Anglo-American. Many individuals or groups have concluded that they have not been given a fair chance, so there is no use in making an effort. Even when many opportunities have been open to minorities through affirmative action, rent subsidies, and entitlement programs, many are reluctant to take advantage of them, which is perplexing.

On the other hand, there are others from the same social groups who say they would rather not have assistance because they are so dynamic that they know that they will achieve their goals no matter what obstacles should appear . . . and they do make it on their own. Many immigrants who come to this country with far more obstacles to overcome, such as cultural and language barriers, seem to do better than minorities who are born in this country. As an example, one in twelve Asian households have an income of less than $15,000 per year when they first come to this country. Within five years, one in seven of these same households has an income of over $50,000 per year. The success of these people contradicts the theory that only the white Anglo can succeed and achieve the American dream. The difference seems to be not in ability but in *attitude*. The Asians, for example, see opportunity or possibility rather than being pessimistic or thinking impossibility thoughts.

Shakespeare said that life is our stage and we are all actors. This is so true. Life is a stage and we tend to act out the scripts we have been told to play. One way or the other, your life is a continuous series of scenes in a play. The play must go on until you die. The only control you have over your life, the play, is changing the script. You can write a new script at any time. All it takes is a conscious decision to accept a new attitude.

ATTRACTING GOOD LUCK

Have you ever wondered why certain people seem to be lucky? What is this thing called luck? Can you acquire it? How do you acquire it? Most people have no idea what luck really is. They try to attract luck, to draw its force for an instant here and an instant there, hoping that it will bring them what they want. Most people's attitude about luck is a mixture of rationalization, resignation, and superstition. In truth, you are already a winner, but you must learn to control your life and destiny. When you do, your personality, instinct, and intuition will attract, recognize, and respond to favorable turns of events.

How do we do this? The good news is that in order to experience good luck you do not have to change who you are. In fact, you are so unique that *you cannot change who you are,* even if you tried. It is important that you get the idea that there is nothing wrong with you. There is nothing wrong with being who you are. If that is true, you are only left with one option. You must change the way you look at things or your perception of reality.

STOP UNLUCKY PATTERNS

Negative patterns, or bad-luck patterns, must be stopped. They must be stopped consciously. First of all, never complain about your bad luck, because nobody really cares but you. Other people's exaggerated memories of their own bad luck dwarf whatever you are complaining about. In some cases, if you complain about your bad luck to others, they can actually be *inspired* by your being unlucky. They may even try to take advantage of you when you are down on your luck because they think you are weak or you are not a force to be reckoned with.

If you consider yourself a poor, unlucky loser who always gets the bad end of everything, you will attract more of the same. If you see yourself as a victim, you will always be a victim. In truth, most victims are really volunteers. We volunteer by being unconscious or unaware. This sets us up for the bad luck cycles we experience in life.

By believing in yourself and your ability to attract good luck, you will set a new momentum that will change and amaze you. The stronger your belief, the greater the success, but you have to desire it and act on it, not just wish for it. The greater your desire and willingness to act, the greater the power you have over your life. It requires an *unwavering* belief that you are *already* lucky. Lucky people get lucky breaks. They get the promotions, win, enjoy financial and social success, and have healthy, happy relationships.

LUCK IS NOT RANDOM

If you think luck is random, you are wrong. This can be demonstrated by the consistency of lucky and unlucky persons. Consistently unlucky people suffer from a lack of focus, apathy, and low self-esteem. They set themselves up as victims of circumstances. It appears that luck is pushing them one way and then another. Their view of life is that they are unlucky. They keep attracting more bad luck, so they keep reinforcing their belief. They think unlucky, they act unlucky, they speak unlucky, and therefore they are unlucky.

STATE OF MIND, STATE OF LUCK

The question remains: Can you really attract good luck? Is it possible to develop skills whereby you can fairly well control the particular outcome of events in your life? Can you, with concerted effort, really change your luck? Can you, in truth, control your destiny, or is this just positive thinking nonsense? The answer is, no, this is not nonsense. It is a sound psychological principle.

It is my contention that to acquire and maintain good luck, you do not have to make any drastic change in your life. All efforts to improve your job, marriage, relationship, health, or money are useless. They mean nothing if you persist in believing that the worst will happen or that you are an unlucky person who gets all of life's bad breaks. Trying to change your outer experiences before changing your inner beliefs is a total waste of time and energy. Without changing your attitude first, the new job, marriage, divorce, a move, health, relationships, money—all of it—will still leave you with an empty feeling. What is worse, even if you get what you want, you will lose it because your belief is that you are a loser and unlucky.

Once you have mastered the mental adjustments, you will open yourself up to intuition and hunches that you can profit from. Lucky people are often guided by intuition and hunches. If used effectively, they can be extremely useful and lucrative. Hunches are based on a reservoir of subconscious facts that you have accumulated over a period of time. To develop intuition and hunches, you must access what you know. If you have a background in a certain area and you get a strong hunch, more than likely you will be correct. We are not talking about hunches that are random bits of irrelevancy, but those that are based on some realization from your past experiences. You cannot trust a hunch unless you have some background in that situation. For example, if you have no background in the stock market and you get a hunch, it is untrustworthy.

DON'T MAKE THINGS WORSE THAN THEY ARE

You must never worry about whether you are lucky or unlucky. You can't control your luck, but you can control your *decisions* and therefore dramatically affect your luck. Our attitude, or state of mind, determines the decisions we make. One decision determines the next. In the end, we either win or lose. Sometimes we make bad decisions. The important thing is to accept things as they are. Do your best to change them, but don't attract more bad luck by making things worse. I never met anyone who didn't make things worse sometimes, including myself. We get angry, we feel we have been cheated, or that we have lost something, and we try to get even. We lose at romance or business and we make things worse by throwing ourselves out of sync.

This happens all the time in life. For example, we allow a broken relationship to distort and destroy other areas of our lives because we are no longer thinking rationally. Decisions that would normally matter don't seem to matter by comparison. In life, people who are heartbroken often make the worst business decisions imaginable. Those decisions don't seem to matter compared to the heartbreak. Those decisions add up, and eventually, even if they didn't matter so much individually, they will matter in the end. If it doesn't matter now, it will matter tomorrow.

What particularly intensifies this unfavorable state of mind is when we feel heavily invested in certain situations. Many people will stay in a bad relationship, job, or project because they don't want to be wrong and because they have put so much of themselves and their money into whatever it is. This keeps them where they are and even makes things worse. From now on, promise yourself you will never make things worse.

Why is it so hard for us to let go when the signs that are telling us we should do so are so obvious? Because we will not change any situation until the pain of staying where we are is greater than the temporary pain we will experience making the change. Usually, before we take the leap and make a change, our difficult situation tends to seem bigger than life. In retrospect, after we have taken the risk of starting anew, the change we feared has almost always diminished. What we thought was so bad just wasn't so bad after all, or at least we realize we have moved on, leaving a bad situation behind us.

A negative situation may bring about an attitude of self-defeat, impossibility, or failure in one individual or group, but another individual or group will see only possibilities and the opportunity to succeed. If we have a self-defeating attitude, we set ourselves up for continued failure. This is worsened if we insist on blaming external forces and see our failure as an isolated misfortune bestowed upon only us and not others. The kinds of conclusions we draw concerning our impossible situations are key in how we perceive our difficult circumstances, and those conclusions are key in whether we can overcome them. For most of us, it is a matter of giving up too easily by blaming others for our impossible situations.

HOMEOSTASIS—RESISTANCE TO CHANGE

No matter how committed you are to changing your life for the better, there will come a time when you will start backsliding. Is it because you are lazy or have no willpower? Not necessarily. Backsliding is a universal experience. Every one of us resists significant change, whether it is necessarily accepting something less, or even something better. Our body, brain, and behavior have a built-in tendency to stay at the same level and to resist change. This resistance to change is called *homeostasis*. It is characterized in all self-regulating systems, both psychological and physical. A simple example of homeostasis can be found in your home heating system. The thermostat on the wall senses the room temperature. When the temperature drops below the level you set, it turns on the heater. The heater completes the loop by sending heat to the room. When the room reaches the temperature level you set, the thermostat sends an electrical signal back to the heater to turn off the heat, thus retaining homeostasis.

We all have psychological feedback loops. The problem is that they are limited to whatever level we are used to. They keep things as they are, even if things aren't very good. Whenever you make a change, your subconscious feels threatened and starts sending warning messages. This is just part of your survival mechanism. Your subconscious thinks that if you make the change, you won't survive, so it tries to protect you.

Homeostasis doesn't distinguish between change for the better or change for the worse. It resists all change. Even if you enjoy and profit from the change, you will meet with homeostasis sooner or later. You might experience homeostatic alarm signals in the form of physical or psychological symptoms. You might unconsciously sabotage yourself. Even though you want to win, you will find yourself losing at things where you should have easily won. For this reason, it is important to reset your level of homeostasis. The level is determined by your values and goals, and then by reprogramming them into the subconscious so the subconscious can reset the automatic homeostatic level.

THE POWER OF INSTANT REPLAY— PREPLAY IT

Resetting your homeostatic level is quite simple. Most of us are familiar with the term *instant replay*. A video camera records what has happened and is able to play back an event for review. Unfortunately, when watching a replay, there is nothing we can do to change what has happened.

Several years ago, I began teaching a concept that I call *instant preplay*. It is the opposite of instant replay. Using instant preplay, we record an incident in our mind before it happens. It is a demonstrated fact that we are teleological, which means we move toward what we picture. Physically, emotionally, and psychologically we create what we picture in our mind by visualizing it with activity and movement.

The best way for imagery to work is that it must be in the first person, present tense, and it should have movement. This is accomplished by putting yourself in the picture with repetitive involvement. You must see yourself having already accepted the outcome. It then becomes the job of your subconscious to get the picture to match your reality. (In Gestalt psychology this is called *closure*.)

As the new picture becomes more vivid with repetition, the subconscious is compelled to supply the means to make the image a reality. It does this by alerting you to the necessary people, places, and events that will assist you in achieving your goal. Your subconscious will also supply the creative energy and drive to accomplish the end result. This creates your new level of homeostasis.

The total quality and quantity of your life is determined by what you preplay in your mind. Instead of using instant replay, which focuses on the past, start using instant preplay and create your future the way you want it.

ANCHOR YOUR BRAIN TO SUCCESS

The concept of anchoring is used extensively by the advertising media. They anchor your brain to a specific logo (such as McDonald's arches with their name), certain colors (like Kodak's yellow packaging), and music (with AT&T using Whitney Houston's "True Voice"). Such stimuli trigger our brains to think about the advertising message and reminds us to purchase the product. We can use these kinds of trigger techniques to our advantage.

As many of you know, I am an avid thoroughbred handicapper. Before I open the *Racing Form,* I look at the *Racing Form* logo on the front page and say, "My brain guides me to the winner in each race." Since our subconscious mind is a cybernetic mechanism, every time I look at the *Daily Racing Form* logo, it triggers a winning pattern recognition. By using this triggering technique the brain will, at the right moment, intuitively seek out the best information from past strategies that produced success. All of our senses create such triggers in our brains: sight, smell, touch, taste, sound, and even our sixth sense (our intuition) responds.

If advertisers are willing to invest millions so that they can anchor our brains to think of their products or services, it only makes sense that we can do the same. I know it works because I am a winner.

However, don't take my word for it. Do it for yourself. It only takes a few seconds, and the results will far outweigh the effort.

IMAGINATION GENERATES NEW POSSIBILITIES

There are numerous techniques for creating positive images that bring winning results. The degree to which we assume something is possible or impossible is largely controlled by our imagination. As one of the most powerful, creative tools at our disposal, the imagination is continuously active and only we can govern whether our selective imaging is positive or negative.

When we use the imagination negatively by reliving the pains of the past (fears, guilt, and feelings of anger or unworthiness), we automatically limit our circle of possibility. Our imagination not only replays the negative images of the past, but it replays them in a larger and more detailed manner than they actually occurred. Even small failures become monumental disasters. The original damage is magnified, since our subconscious plays its natural role by accepting these elaborate images as actual experience. The subconscious proceeds to keep us in a prison of negativity by implementing similar experiences to coincide with this understanding of reality. In essence, we create an unhappy, insecure present by picturing past sadness and perceived failure, and then we try to form our future from a present state of mind that is built upon those negative images of the past. As long as we let our imagination focus on an unworkable past, we are unable to move into a self-sustaining future. Using past negative images while trying to visualize a positive future is *completely incompatible.*

You can choose how you are going to use your imagination. It belongs to you, and no one has control over it except for you. You can remember whatever parts of the past you want, and preplay the future you desire. By selectively applying your imagination, you can focus on the positive experiences from your past (there really *are* positive experiences if you will look for them) and use these images to form a solid base for the future. Perceiving a positive future not only shows us how to get where we want to go but actually draws us toward the people, circumstances, places, and conditions to fulfill our image of the future. On the other hand, a negative image of the future also draws us toward the people, places, and events to convince us that what we want is impossible. It's your choice.

Using positive and purposeful imaging offers a radical departure from negative self-talk in affirming a better self created for a positive future. Decide to take responsibility for your current state of reality, and take responsibility for how you choose to operate in it. Take a chance on the new, and expand the potential in your life by selectively imaging the best for yourself. Look at where you are in the present moment and decide concretely where you would most like to be in all areas of your life. Allow your mind to be free. Visualize images for the creation of new possibilities based on these observations, and you will be amazed at the desires that will surface and the creative solutions you will discover to enable effective action. As purposeful, creative beings, positive images provide excitement, direction, and a clear vision for which we will make the best effort. For the highly visual person, this conceptual portion of the possibility process is often deeply satisfying. Certainly, visual validation is a key element in expanding our circle of possibility and defining the potential benefits in enacting change. If you are a person who responds powerfully to the sense of hearing or touch, add these kinds of stimulus to your visualization.

In making choices, people often support the impossibility stance by asserting, "I can't." This is usually based on what they have experienced in the past—the images that they hold in their minds. Of course, this typical disclaimer is sustained by what we tend to think of as good reasons (really excuses) as to why achieving, having, or being a specific something is quite impossible.

The truth of the matter is that you can be, do, or have just about anything you choose. However, if you think something is impossible, or if you don't do a certain thing, it is because you choose to accept it as impossible. *It is not because you can't.* Whenever you get into the "I can't" syndrome, it helps to say to yourself, "I can, but right now I choose not to." At least you are acknowledging that no one or nothing outside of you is controlling you. Any delay in creating what you want is not the result of people, circumstances, or conditions outside of you, but rather your limited circle of possibility. Your circle of possibility can only be expanded through possibility thinking.

CHAPTER 5

Taking Responsibility for
Impossible Situations

Probably the most difficult concept to grasp is the idea that we are fully responsible for all that we experience in our lives. By taking responsibility for our lives and our happiness, we rid ourselves of emotional dependency, and therefore we are self-reliant. Often, we know what the consequences of our actions will be, other times we may not, but either way around, we are responsible for our actions. By taking the stance of being fully responsible, we enrich our lives by finding better, more responsible solutions.

Psychologist Albert Ellis states: "The best years of your life are the ones in which you decide your problems are your own. You don't blame them on your mother, the ecology, or the President. You realize that you control your own destiny." When we face crises we tend to see life and all that happens around us differently. We can become bitter as we blame everyone or everything around us, or we can become more aligned with our purpose and our Greater Self as we heighten our approach to life.

Ultimately, we would see that we are responsible for our own life . . . our own experiences. The forces of change bring us opportunities that allow us to refocus on our life purpose and see more clearly that we are responsible for our own fulfillment and happiness.

NINETY-NINE PERCENT
ACCOUNTABILITY DOESN'T WORK

The difficult, but most important step, is taking accountability for where we are right now. As long as we deny being responsible for our life being the way it is, as long as we blame society, parents, our mate, friends, family, the government, our employer, or anyone else, we put our power to change our life beyond our reach. If we deny even 1 percent, that 1 percent adds and multiplies every day. The only way we can move from an impossible to a possible situation is to be totally accountable at all times. Notice that I didn't say most of the time, or

50 percent of the time. If you are not accountable all the time, then it sets you up as the victim for the times you choose to not be accountable. This is selective accountability.

One of the quotes in my *THINK* book is, "There are no victims, only volunteers." With the exception of children or the mentally incompetent, I believe no one can do it to us unless we give them permission or unless we set ourselves up to be victims. Another quote in the book is, "If you are being mistreated, you are cooperating with the treatment."

Those who see themselves as victims are outraged. I have received letters from people citing example after example about how their circumstances are different. It really wasn't their fault. Perhaps they're right . . . and perhaps they are wrong. However, there is one major problem with this line of reasoning. If they are not accountable, who is? Once we make something external accountable for our experience, then our life is about getting them to change. What are the odds of that happening? Usually, slim to none. Once again, when we blame others, we get to be right, but we still don't have what we want. Being accountable allows us to learn from our past and move into the future.

ACCOUNTABILITY IS NOT SELF-BLAME

I am not saying we should blame ourselves for what has happened, but we must realize that in some way we participated in the end result, either consciously or unconsciously. At this point comes the why or the how question. We can either say, "Why did this happen to me?" or "How can I change my attitude, behavior, and actions so that it will be better in the future?" Notice we didn't say, "How can I get them to change?" but "How can I change and self-correct?"

It is easy to fall into the trap of the victim. When we see people who lose their homes in a flood, hurricane, or earthquake, we sympathize with them. However, the bottom line is that they are still accountable for what has happened. They are accountable not for the hurricane, flood, or earthquake but for living in a high-risk area. It is a known fact that hurricanes occur in the Southeast. It is a known fact that the levees in the Midwest can burst whenever there is too much rain. It is a known fact that California is on an earthquake fault. Yet, people still choose to live in these areas of the country.

There is nothing wrong with that, but they are accountable for their decision to live with the risk factor. They are accountable for their choices, even though they appear to be victims. I recently read a government report that most people who live in high-risk areas don't carry insurance. Earthquake and flood insurance is relatively inexpensive, yet they refuse to accept that a major natural disaster can occur, and when it does, they truly believe they are victims.

You might argue that there are a few exceptions. Sometimes things happen to people and there just seems to be no reason for it. There was no way they could have avoided it. Even if we acknowledge that there are a few exceptions where people are true victims of their circumstances, let's say 5 percent, the problem is that 95 percent of the population thinks they are in that 5 percent. Of course, 95 percent of the population remain in impossible situations. The interesting thing about life is that we've always got to be right.

How do you feel when you are around people who tell you their story of victimization with no intention of making the changes they know are necessary in order to resolve the problem? These seasoned victims have it down to a science. They blame, complain, moan, and groan. The longer they tell it and the more people they tell it to, the better they are at eliciting a response. The worst part is that they want to drag you down with them. It makes you want to shake them awake. If they are not going to do anything about their predicament, they are not victims, they are volunteers. Once these people stop volunteering, their lives will change.

Unfortunately, many people like being victims. It becomes a way of life. It not only keeps them from being accountable for their experiences, but it gives them something to talk about. In fact, some of these people would have nothing to say if they weren't complaining. These people are eventually perceived as pain symbols to everyone they come in contact with.

We like to be around people who are positive and accountable for whatever they experience and for whatever they do. However, no one wants to be around a pain symbol. These are the type of people that brighten up a room when they leave. Don't be one of them. Notice how you feel when you are around people who take charge of their lives and focus on how they can make life better. These are the people we want to associate with because they encourage us to be accountable.

YOU CAN'T CONTROL THE
EXTERNAL, SO CONTROL YOUR
INTERNAL

We must approach life from the standpoint that our life will either be controlled externally or internally. If you have been an external type of blamer, you attribute your failures on childhood, poor education, poverty, or feeling you have never been given a chance. On the other hand, if you are the internal type, you recognize that you are in charge of your life, accountable for the results as well as the lack of results, and you know that you have the power to make the changes that will improve any situation. Work hard at eliminating your own complaints about things you can do nothing to change, and do something about the things you can change.

Our society has become a mass of external types. Collectively, we have become a society of blamers and helpless victims. This is reinforced by the media, and of particular note, the recent increase in TV talk shows has dramatically boosted this phenomenon. The shows feature guests suffering from every imaginable condition, and what is worse, they portray these individuals as helpless victims of some external misfortune. The focus of the programs tends to be on how we need to change those external causes of our problems so that others won't suffer the same fate.

If an external source is not the cause of their problems, then the shows convey that they must be suffering from some type of mental disease that justifies their behavior. If drinking or drugs has ruined their lives, the cause is not a lack of self-control, but the disease of alcoholism and the addiction to drugs. If they gamble and lose their money, the reason is that they are compulsive gamblers. If they have a high sex drive, they are sex addicts. If they are violent, then it is because their parents were either too strict or not strict enough, but whichever it is, it is never the right amount of control from the parents. There is an excuse for every deviant behavior you can think of. As if these presentations aren't enough, the shows bring in an expert in the chemical or biological field to tell us that it isn't their fault; the real problem is too much sugar, caffeine, or poor nutrition.

IT'S NOT MY FAULT

As I wrote this, I was reading in *USA Today* about a woman in Florida who won an $11 million lawsuit against Kmart because her husband purchased a rifle while he was intoxicated. It is outrageous that there was a legal claim filed against the store maintaining that the clerk was at fault because he did not correctly determine the physical and mental condition of the man at the time of the sale. The man shot his wife. Was this was Kmart's fault? If we take this premise a step further, then the real culprit here would be the distributor who sold the gun to Kmart. If they hadn't sold the gun to Kmart, this would not have happened. Really, though, it is the manufacturer of the rifle. If they had not made the gun, none of this would have happened. I think you get the point.

This logic is about as logical as saying flies cause garbage. The issue here is not to blame the stores who sell guns or the manufacturers of guns. The issue is the responsibility of the individual who got drunk. He is totally responsible for his conduct, especially when he injures another person. And we are fully responsible for ourselves and our conduct. Still, the continuing message on these talk shows is that what happens to people is not their fault, and if they do something to harm themselves or others, there is always some external factor involved that was beyond their control. Clearly, it is time to stop this nonsense.

REPEAT IT UNTIL YOU GET IT

How many times have we discovered that we keep repeating the same thing over and over again? Even in relationships, the names and faces change, but the relationship problems are the same. The reason for this is that we keep doing things the same way as we have always done them. This repetition sets us up to experience the same outcome.

One method that you can use to prevent having the same kind of relationships over and over again is to make a list of various people that you have been close to in your life, particularly love relationships. Then list all the types of problems that occurred, and list the characteristics of the other party that you had difficulty with. You also might note what unfavorable characteristics came out in you as well. You can note a pattern in the characteristics and problems that arose in your relationships and see how you might be attracting the same type of people and experiences over and over again. Knowing what you have been attracting will help you move on with a fresh start in your relationships and in your life experiences.

Practice new techniques for responding to people with the characteristics that have been difficult for you to handle in the past so you can stop making the same mistakes. Even if another person might be a bully, you must still learn and practice the response that will diffuse such encounters. Ultimately, your love relationship and any other kinds of relationships will improve or change so that you will not attract those problems again. In addition, you will not attract people in your life who have characteristics that are not workable for you. If someone comes along whom you know you would not get along with, you'll avoid getting involved with the person as soon as you see the red flags that tell you to avoid that person. Make the changes; if you keep *doing* what you have been *doing,* you will keep *getting* what you have been *getting*.

The only authority figure is within yourself. When you look internally rather than externally for who or what is responsible for your success, you realize that you—*only you*—know the truth about what is working and what is not working for you. When you are honest with yourself, you can clearly see what needs to be adjusted in order to successfully get what you want in life. On the other hand, if you allow others to make decisions for you, they will surely end up doing it *to* you.

CHANGE FROM THE INSIDE OUT

All permanent and lasting change must come from the inside out. The way you are is *not* the result of what has happened to you, it's the result of what you decide to *keep inside* you. For most people, it is a matter of trying to change things from the outside in, changing the circumstance and conditions first. The belief is that if something outside of us changes, then we will be happy. Rarely will changing anything outside of ourselves change our life on a permanent and lasting basis. Rearranging our outside circumstances just wastes valuable time and energy, because the underlying cause, our thought processes and choices, has not changed. It's like rearranging deck chairs on the *Titanic*. The ship is going down, no matter how you arrange the scenery.

This avoidance behavior is similar to driving down the road and noticing that your gas gauge is on empty. Instead of doing something about it, you choose to ignore it by putting your hand over the gas gauge and pretending it's full. By denying accountability and refusing to take action, you remain in the status quo of impossibility. As you do this, the circumstances of your life journey continue to worsen. You will slowly run out of gas. Is it possible that you are about to run out of gas if you don't pull over and fill up soon?

This is not to say that our past does not influence our future, but our past will not control our future unless we let it. You may not be responsible for your past, but you are in charge of your future. The key is to move forward, or as Captain Picard of the *Star Trek* ship *Enterprise* says, "Make it so."

Unfortunately, no instruction manuals were provided when we came to this planet. Most of our instruction about how to handle our life has come from outside sources. This has caused us to disengage our internal learning mechanism. We go through life with a set of unworkable beliefs and values. It's no wonder why things keep happening to us. Rather than reassessing our beliefs and values, most people tend to focus on rationalizing, justifying, defending, and trying to look good. The result is that it consumes our energy to change and blocks our ability to find new solutions. When a problem arises, we need to look for possibilities and view them as opportunities for new solutions. This was best said by William Bridges: "Genuine beginnings begin within us, even when they are brought to our attention by external opportunities."

"HOW CAN I" VS. "WHY ME"
QUESTIONS

If you won't take responsibility for all that you experience, you will not release the parts of you that need to go, and you will stay stuck in your own rut. The act of *releasing* is vital in order for you to be free of excess baggage that could keep you from having the happiness and success you want. If you spend all of your time blaming all your problems on things outside of yourself and asking *"Why* me?" rather than looking at "How can I?" to solve your own problems, you will fail to succeed in life. Remember, this is true even if the only reason you may have attracted a negative experience is because it's just another lesson for you. It is still your experience and therefore your responsibility.

When a negative experience occurs, ask yourself *how* you can change your thinking, your method, or your behavior to turn things around for the better. The way we ask ourselves questions either moves us toward or away from the solution. "Why me" questions move us away from solutions. When we ask this kind of question, we assume that something outside of us is the cause of our experience. For example, "Why did this happen to me? Why me, God? Why do they always do that? Why don't they leave me alone?" Every time we ask ourselves "why me" questions, we are wasting valuable energy because there are no answers. These are endless loop questions that keep us going in circles. Usually one "why me" question leads to another.

"How can I" questions, on the other hand, are based on the assumption that we are the cause of our own experience and results. We are seeking answers that will lead us to *results* instead of *reasons*. For example, "How can I make this better? How can I do this? How can I change that? How can I make a positive difference?" Did you notice the difference in thought? The "why me" questions make us unaccountable and set us up as victims. The "how can I" questions make us accountable and ready to take action. "How can I" questions do something wonderful for us, as they open us up to possibility thinking. Asking ourselves how opens our minds to our unlimited creative resources as we ask ourselves, "How can I *create* a positive result?" Notice all the how questions shown above demonstrate a personal request for a creative action.

So we need to get the "why me" stuff out of our heads. The movie character, Forrest Gump, quoted his mother as saying, "Life is like a box of chocolates. Ya' never know what yer gonna git." In an interview with the actor who played Forrest Gump, Tom Hanks said, "This is horrifyingly so." And, wouldn't you think Hanks would have it all, including plenty of money to solve all his problems? Yet he termed it *"horrifyingly"* so. There is no room in our minds for all the "why me" dwelling that we tend to do. We have unlimited answers for "how can I" to get what we want in life. Once you see the "how can I" questions as unlimited, you will see life is filled with unlimited opportunity and pleasure.

CHANGING TO "I CAN" THINKING

There are only two things you have to do in life. You have to die, and you have to live until you die. You make up all the rest. It's up to you to decide in your *mind* what you can do.

It's never too late to change the way we think. Letting go is not easy, but it could be easier to let go if we would just practice by saying, "Yes! I can see this a different way." "Yes! I can change the way I do this." Like Nancy Reagan's antidrug campaign, "Just say no," just say "Yes, I will!" I love the children's story of *The Little Engine That Could.* This is what the train sounds out as it choo-choos along: "I *think* I can, I *think* I can, I *think* I can." It's a choice that we can make regarding being open and positive about how we perceive what we can do.

Our emotions affect how we record occurrences in our brain. In other words, our brain records what it *thinks* (or feels and believes) is happening. We can affect our emotions by using self-talk to direct our brain in the manner in which we want it to believe. This is facilitated by putting together *words* and *pictures* in order to bring about the *emotions* we prefer.

It has taken all our lives for our brains to get programmed to the point where we are right now, and yet we can change our programming far more quickly than we realize. Just imagine yourself being a tape recorder. When you are recording, the tape runs in real time, but think how fast the tape runs when you hit rewind. Then you can record right over the old stuff . . . all the new, positive, possibility thinking you select.

Nobody is telling you that you have to do anything with the way you think or what you do. It is *you* that has the choice to simply say, "I can do what I put my mind to do." If you think you *have* to, you won't. This is a natural tendency. You have power when you say to yourself that you *can* do whatever you set out to do. When you make a commitment to yourself and others, you are as strong as your word is strong.

A perfect story of undying commitment is that of the University of Notre Dame football player about which a movie has been made in his name, *Rudy.* This fellow really didn't quite have the physical ability to make the team, much less get a chance on the playing field, yet it was his dream, and he worked hard to get it. He worked so hard at his dream that the entire Notre Dame team rallied their support and demanded that the coach put Rudy in the game for a while. The crowd in the football stadium got wind of what was going on and the stadium then echoed a repetitive cheer for Rudy to be allowed to play in the game of the season. When Rudy got his chance to play, he made an outstanding tackle. No one since has ever been lifted up by their cheering team and carried off the field.

SHORT-TERM BENEFITS, LONG-TERM RISK

We all know that alcohol, smoking, and drugs are potentially destructive. The harm that can come from them is foreseeable. In fact, every package of cigarettes contains a warning. Why do people smoke? The primary reason is that it makes the smoker feel good. This is also true of other harmful habits such as alcohol, drugs, gambling, and overexposure to the sun while getting a tan.

The other reason people smoke cigarettes is that it helps them escape awareness of themselves. Nervous people find that smoking gives them something to do with their hands. The benefits are immediate and the costs are apparent but come much later. Drinking tonight may make you feel good, but the hangover doesn't come until tomorrow morning, and the liver damage or marital and family breakup doesn't come until much later. Cigarettes offer immediate pleasure, but the cost and problems don't come until much later. Having a tan makes you look and feel good, but prematurely wrinkled and dried skin or possible skin cancer don't show up until later in life. Substance abuse fits the pattern of accepting long-term costs to gain immediate satisfaction.

SHORT-TERM EMOTIONAL RELIEF, LONG-TERM PAIN

Just as is the case with self-destructive physical behaviors such as smoking or drug abuse, short-term emotional relief always comes at the cost of increased risk of long-term psychological, emotional, and physical damage. By not taking responsibility for what we do, we merely forestall an inevitable confrontation with pain and reality.

THE INVESTMENT MENTALITY

Often we refuse to take responsibility for investing our money, time, or effort in something that isn't working because we won't give up the investment mentality. Too many people end up being losers because they try to recover what they have lost rather than responding to new opportunities that arise at the same time.

In life, it doesn't matter how much money, time, or effort you have invested in your relationships, business, or real estate, there are times when you must let go and begin anew. As Kenny Rogers said in "The Gambler," "You have to know when to hold 'em and know when to fold 'em." When we take responsibility for our circumstances, no matter what, we command our own success because we more readily dump whatever is flawed and quickly move on with a better plan.

Sometimes we are so invested in what happens to us that we put far too much effort into the situation. Then, after the crisis has subsided, we find that the extra effort made no difference whatsoever. Things would have worked out in the same positive manner without all the extra effort and stress. Of course, it's important to cover all your bases by making sure details are handled, but if you operate out of fear and become obsessive about every detail, you might end up stressing yourself out and losing ground by being too pushy with those around you. Granted, these days, in all the rush and hurry, people make errors while they handle some of our matters for us, but if we get intensely attached to our problems, we can invest much more than is necessary.

TAKING RESPONSIBILITY FOR RISKS

The rewards in life are always in proportion to the risk. This is true of investments, business dealings, and personal relationships. The potential cost, loss, or discomfort associated with taking a risk keeps us from making the impossible possible. The truth of the matter is that most of the time the cost, loss, or discomfort of *not* taking risks is a greater price to pay than taking them. Clearly, not taking risks is also our responsibility. How true is this quote of Jim Rohn's: "If you are not willing to risk the unusual, you will have to settle for the ordinary."

Risks fall into many categories including emotional, physical, financial, and spiritual. We are afraid to take risks because we are afraid of being hurt financially, psychologically, or emotionally, but by not taking risks, the only thing we can be assured of is that we will have more of what we had before. For most people, the biggest risk of all is in *not* taking risks.

At least by taking risks we have the opportunity to find out if something is possible for us. This is particularly true of relationships. In a relationship we must risk. The only way to fully experience any relationship is to risk everything. This means allowing yourself to be prepared and able to handle it emotionally if it does not work out, or to experience a greater amount of joy than you have ever experienced before. If we are willing to risk and totally commit, the chances are that the relationship will blossom and will add to the lives of both individuals. Even if it doesn't work, at least you will know for sure that it wasn't right for you, not because of a lack of commitment or risk on your part, but because of other factors.

It is important to understand that often there is no real way of knowing without experiencing. What this means is that you can't know something until you do it. If you have never been in a swimming pool and someone told you about the water and how it feels to swim, there is still no way to know how to swim or how it feels until you jump in and find out for yourself. In doing so, there is a certain risk involved. Life works the same way.

Turning the impossible into the possible requires you to move outside your circle of possibility, beyond your wall of resistance, and there is no way of doing this without taking risks and making a few mistakes. Once you understand this, you set yourself free to explore unlimited possibilities.

MISTAKES ARE JUST PART OF OUR EVERYDAY PERFORMANCE

We make mistakes every day. If you don't make some mistakes every day, then you are not doing enough of the right stuff to succeed. Don't deny your mistakes when they occur or deny that you made an error. If you spend your time trying to cover up your mistakes to yourself or others, you won't take responsibility for making necessary improvements. You do not have to permanently own your mistakes, as they are *not who you are;* they are a temporary occurrence. Certainly, we all need to take responsibility for what we do, but only going as far as admitting it and then moving on. It is easier to say, "Yes, I did that. I see what did not work. Now, what can I do to make things better?"

We all know what it is like to be falsely blamed for something. For example, a boss who is more concerned about whether you respect him than whether you meet his deadlines can cause some serious problems for you when he tries to cover up his mistakes . . . especially by blaming you. You can try to keep the waters calm by constantly building up the boss's belief in your respect, but when he makes another mistake, the inevitable will happen. Don't you be like the boss I just described. That person will get caught at the game sooner or later. Business and people are much more aware and tuned in to authenticity than to let people get away with such tricky behavior.

Corporations have become increasingly supportive of risk taking, trying new things and believing that people should *not* be degraded for making mistakes. They believe that any failed attempts in new methods tried while working on projects should be accepted as part of the path to achieving excellence. If this is so, why should we be disappointed in ourselves when we make mistakes? The only kind of disappointment should be that the method tried did not work. How disappointing it is when people try to cover up their mistakes, making matters worse. If you are quick to acknowledge your mistake, you can make everything better right away by shifting your plan. Risk taking is an acceptable way to try new things. If you make a mistake, you should *not* feel guilty.

NOT NOW—MAYBE LATER

Your effectiveness as a person can be measured by your ability to complete things. Incomplete and unresolved elements of life drain our resources and waste our creative energy. The energy of avoidance is substituted for creative energy. Some of us have multiple sources of energy drainers in relationships, business, unpaid debts, keeping agreements, and withholding love and appreciation. All of this keeps us living in the past while diminishing our present. The best way to escape from your past or current problems is to solve them.

Procrastination comes about because we think completing or

changing something will be more difficult than not doing it. In other words, we tend to perceive that the payoff for staying where we are outweighs the benefits we will experience if we do something about it. As we know, unless the perceived pleasure is greater than the pain we think making a change would bring us, we will not change. Add procrastination to the factor, and we are doubling our resistance to success. How willing is a procrastinator to change habits? *Procrastination is the fault most people put off correcting.*

Why do we procrastinate? Usually we prefer the immediate benefits of having fun or doing whatever we feel like, rather than being willing to pay the price of getting the work done. Also, we often put off starting a task when we feel we might fail. When our ship comes in, we need to make sure we are willing to unload it. A change in attitude would turn *dread* into getting *ahead*. It might amaze us to find that working on what we really need to work on is actually quite fulfilling. Often, we procrastinate and resist doing a task, and yet once we get started, we actually enjoy it. Certainly, we enjoy the satisfaction of completing it at the very least. It is impossible to *win* unless you *begin*. Many of us spend our whole lives waiting for our ship to come in. The problem is, we never sent one out.

DON'T HANG ON TO SINKING SHIPS

A friend of mine who is a stockbroker shared an interesting statistic with me. He said that a study performed by one of the major investment companies showed that over 85 percent of investors persist beyond the point when they first become aware they should get out of an investment that potentially is ready to decline in value. Even more interesting is the fact that over 50 percent persisted beyond the break-even point of their original investment. This is the point at which getting out of the investment would bring back less than their initial investment.

A perfect example of this self-destructive and fruitless behavior is the U.S. government. It continues to pour millions of dollars into projects that are doomed to failure. The advantage that the government has over you and me is that it can disregard the consequences because all it has to do is raise taxes to pay for continued and persistent failures. The taxpayers, on the other hand, will eventually run out of money.

People often persist in impossible situations because of an investment mentality. They have time, money, emotional, and psychological investment in a person, business situation, property, stock, or whatever, and they don't want to lose their investment. This can be seen in situations where people are willing to throw good money after bad. Once we feel we have an investment in something, we are reluctant to abandon our investment or previous efforts. The downside is that we squander what we have left rather than only losing what we already have invested.

We are programmed to believe that to back out after we have committed time, emotions, energy, or money is to admit failure. Instead of losing what we have invested with little to show for our efforts, we would rather invest more of ourselves in a sinking ship. The hope or illusion is that things will eventually turn around. Often this leads to further failure and puts us into a greater impossible situation.

CHAOS TRIGGERS UNIQUE POSSIBILITIES

Chaos kicks our minds into possibility thinking gear, but why do we tend to be more afraid of the possibilities that could lead us to success than we are of a terrible current situation? It's all anticipatory anxiety. When we calm down, we realize it is not as bad as we fantasized. It's like pulling a bad tooth. All the festering wounds of a bad job or a business relationship—the disappointments, the resentments—are gone in one clean yank, and we are free. After years of accumulating problems and swallowing our anger, we have the chance to begin again.

When we begin again, we are open to new possibilities, which will start coming to us rapidly when we are ready for them. All we need to do is notice them. Have you ever experienced occasions when things just keep falling into place in perfect time? For example, if someone is in sales and she is planning her day, deciding who to call on, and out of the blue a prospective client comes to mind, then she can act on that intuitive impulse, and coincidentally, the client has a huge project that the salesperson wins. Or suppose you decide you want to make a career change, and out of the blue, you get a call from a friend of a friend who can help you.

I remember a professional speaker who said that all she has to do is start making more calls for more work, and she gets business . . . not necessarily from the specific calls she makes, but instead, she *receives* calls from other directions. She believes her burning desire for business attracts the possibilities. C. G. Jung, the noted psychiatrist, termed the phenomenon of the universe just making things fall into their perfect place as *synchronicity*. In the book called *The Artist's Way,* Julia Cameron says of Jung, "Following his own inner leading brought him to experience and describe a phenomenon that some of us prefer to ignore: the possibility of an intelligent and responsive universe, acting and reacting in our interests."

UNDERSTANDING CHAOTIC ORDER

All of this seeming chaos in the world is actually chaotic order. It is a wealth of information and possibilities unfolding in perfect time for us to respond. Why is it so hard for us to remember this when things get hectic? Things can change so drastically, and so fast. As the musical group, The Eagles, described it in the following song, "Take care of your own, because one day they're here, next day they're gone." But *all* is not really gone. Something good will always follow anything that has been bad. Chaos gives us the opportunity to *let go* of all that we don't want anymore. It gives us a lot to work with, whether we realize it or not, at just the right time. Because chaos is fast-paced, it helps us let go of the past that we no longer need, since we are forced to act quickly.

If someone's home burns down, all the necessary tasks keep his mind off of the losses, the memories, and the pain, as he is forced to move on with additional responsibilities. True, going to the site to pick up any remaining things would bring up memories and pain, but during that process, the person may have insights from being there that trigger ideas for finding a fresh home. Maybe someone he is talking to about current matters will give him a tip on a great new home that is nicer than the one he previously had.

Chaos helps us change the way we think because it happens rapidly, and chaos helps us discover *who we are* when everything comes at us at once. Chaos forces us to reach deep within ourselves, to our Greater Self, and it forces us to expand our circle of possibility as we stretch ourselves to new heights. Whatever we thought was the truth may now no longer be the truth for us. Like I've said before, it's great to have a sound foundation of thoughts and beliefs, but we must be willing to dump any belief instantly as soon as we receive any new bit of information that is more valid. We cannot hold conflicting beliefs in our mind without anxiety or distress; something's got to give.

Have you ever noticed how some people will spend their time desperately holding on to their current reality while grasping for every bit of support data they can find so that they *prove they are right?* Sometimes we hold on to opinions, attitudes, and beliefs that are no longer relevant because we are afraid to be proven wrong. We must ask ourselves if we are blocking out new information that may be more relevant and decide what is *truly* correct in each situation.

CLAIMING RESPONSIBILITY FOR BOTH THE GOOD AND THE BAD

We can observe the undesirable personality styles in other people and easily see how negative styles block their success. Consider the person who needs to be right, who has to have *control;* the person who creates drama in his or her life, who has to be emotionally supported while creating *chaos;* the person who has to feel superior, who is always trying to get you to put notches in his or her belt; or the person who thrives on rage, who wants to *get even.* These personality traits can dominate our lives, as they are an underlying force that motivates people in their decision making and affects all their relationships. If we don't take responsibility for our emotional behaviors and realize how they negatively impact our lives (and the lives of those around us), the damages, frustration, and unhappiness will continue to repeat itself.

We would be so much better off if we could notice every small bit of evidence that helps us see ourselves more clearly, more truly. Try being what might seem *overly* sensitive for a switch, and see just how much you may be doing things and saying things in order to satisfy your emotional ego's needs. We all do it to some degree. Even our voice tones and inflections can tell us what we need to know about our personality style and finally help us to get rid of what is undesirable. Get rid of the Created Self that we developed over time because we thought others expected us to act or live a certain way or because we were fearful that others would discover our mistakes or take what we wanted.

Taking responsibility for all you do and all you are involved in does not mean that you must become so strongly attached to everything that you try to overcontrol. You can operate with some degree of personal *detachment* and still be fully *engaged* by putting your passion into your work. Keep in mind that nothing you do is right or wrong, good or bad. It is only *wise* or *unwise*. Give yourself the right to make mistakes, because it is through mistakes that your awareness is expanded. The more self-aware we are, the better we will be at expanding our potential and achieving our Greater Self. Being selfish, being a grouch, or blaming others only makes us and those around us miserable.

What an inspiration it is to look at the Miss America, Heather Whitestone, who is deaf. She is so fresh, bright, inspired, and *capable* of doing whatever she puts her heart into. Heather could have easily made excuses for not doing much of anything with her life, but instead she has achieved the impossible American dream. It took her six years to learn to say her name, she performs superb ballet to music she cannot hear, and the list goes on. Heather excels in a multitude of skills and human qualities, which is why she was chosen to be Miss America. If she could stay positive, so can we all. There is no excuse for being unkind or selfish.

Heather's tips for success are: be positive, believe in your dreams, continually educate yourself, face obstacles, work hard, and build a support team. Notice that all of these tips involve reaching out, taking yourself beyond where you are. If we are rigid in our thinking, as our minds tend to be, we block the flow of new thought. Being more flexible and spontaneous in our thinking is the key. We must practice changing our habits and avoid overcriticizing ourselves and others to the point of judgment. Don't deny your flaws; accept them, fix them, and move on. Take risks and allow yourself to make mistakes, accepting them as just part of life. People who are differently abled, as it is called now, tend to accept their present reality and work with what they've got as they strive for what they want. If they can do it, so can everyone.

Replace your negative images of yourself by identifying and appreciating your own unique talents and gifts. If something distasteful or horrible has happened, *you* are *not* distasteful or horrible. You can fix these things. Turn off your critical internal voice and turn that voice into a friendly, helpful force. Use your internal wisdom and intuition as you identify your values and recommit to them.

CHAPTER 6

Death

The Ultimate Impossible Situation

If you will live as though every day were your last day on earth—someday you will be *right!*

—DR. ROBERT ANTHONY, *THINK*

There is one impossible situation that we must consider before we make plans, goals, and other important life decisions that will affect our lives, and that is our inevitable death. Take it easy, it'll be good for you, I promise.

IS THERE LIFE BEFORE DEATH?

If we seriously considered our inevitable end (on this earth plane, for now), we probably would do things differently. When we consider transcendence, all that we hold dear may not be of the utmost importance in the end. What's worse is that we may spend our lives intensely attached to what we think is important, only to find that when we face death, we may have missed the real importance of life.

Death isn't just about aging or being terminally ill or having a fatal accident, it's also about the little deaths we experience throughout our lives: little deaths of parts of ourselves, little deaths of things or people we had to leave behind. Everyone experiences little deaths, and sometimes large deaths, throughout their lives. Even if your life has run smoothly, and you have been rather free of impossible situations, the one you can't avoid is the inevitability of death.

Physicist John A. Wheeler, known for his work regarding black holes, states, "Life without death is meaningless . . . a picture without a frame." And the famed theologian Paul Tillich asks, "If one is not able to die, is he really able to live?" Contemplating our lives from the perspective of eventual death from time to time can play an important part in giving our lives greater meaning.

This is profoundly exemplified by novelist Muriel Spark, whose character says, "If I had my life over again, I should form the habit of nightly composing myself to thoughts of death. I would practice, as it were, the remembrance of death. There is no other practice which so intensifies life. Death . . . should be part of the full expectancy of life. Without an ever-present sense of death life is insipid. You might as well live on the whites of eggs."

LITTLE DEATHS AND NEAR DEATH EXPERIENCES

People who have had near death experiences, people who have come close to and survived dying, have numerous feelings after coming back to life. Some feel anger at being revived, others are ecstatic in the glory of it all. As they approach their lives again, they reassess their affairs and life goals with a more philosophical approach. They wish to resolve any loose ends with people and settle all their personal affairs. They may speak more freely about their true thoughts. Often, they wish to celebrate life by doing things like taking the vacation they never took. They approach life with a newfound peace and a newfound sense of meaning.

An American writer of the late 1800s, William Ellery Channing, eloquently described the newfound philosophy of those who have had near death experiences. Notice how much of it refers to *quality of life.* "To live with small means, to seek elegance rather than luxury, and refinement rather than fashion; to be worthy, not respectable, and wealthy not rich; to study hard, think quietly, talk gently, act frankly; to listen to stars and birds, to babes and sages with an open heart; to bear all cheerfully, do all bravely, await occasions, hurry never. In a word, to let the spiritual unbidden and unconscious grow up through the common. This is my symphony."

Psychologist and author of *The Fire in the Soul,* Dr. Joan Borysenko, describes the *living* kind of near death experience, when people are challenged with crisis, as follows, *"Dark nights of the soul* are extended periods of dwelling at the threshold when it seems as if we can no longer trust the very ground we stand on, when there is nothing familiar left to hold onto that can give us comfort. If we have a strong belief that our suffering is in the service of growth, dark night experiences can lead us to depths of psychological and spiritual healing and revelation that we literally could not have dreamed of and that are difficult to describe in words without sounding trite."

We have several choices regarding where we go from the dark night. We can suffer a while and then go back to our usual and unsatisfactory habits; we can throw in the towel and self-destruct; or we can make a transition, expanding our circle of possibility, and emerge with courage, insight, and a new drive toward our dreams.

I think that if you just get on with it after a serious problem or series of problems, *without* taking a deep soul-searching look, you will repeat the problem in a similar fashion. You will just go on with a false exterior, perhaps even be a little cocky as a form of self-protection. In contrast, you might take the rough times quite seriously because you realize that you could be gone tomorrow. If each morning, we could really contemplate this, we would have more satisfaction with ourselves and our behavior on a daily basis. If we would center or balance ourselves each morning with preparedness in how we wish to carry ourselves through the day, we would do more admirable things and avoid doing the foolish things.

DEATH—THE REAL
COMPLEMENTARY OPPOSITE

The concept of complementary opposites was previously discussed, regarding our perception of opposites such as good or bad, and happy or sad. The concept of a glass half filled with water can be perceived as half empty or half full. This is a complementary opposite. One thing that certainly intensifies our lives is when we look at the real complementary opposite to life, which is death. If we have spent our whole lives making constant comparisons with what we have and what we don't have, when death faces us, we will surely believe that our life was unhappy.

When we constantly spend our time comparing what we have with something else, we will make our happiness *im*possible. Happiness is a feeling that is held only in the present as our current reality. Where there is *no* comparison, *unhappiness* becomes the impossible. Happiness exists when the mind is not removed from itself, when it remains in the present time zone, and when it declines to contrast itself with other times or conditions.

Happiness is an attitude, a feeling of satisfaction that can only be felt within, by being content with whom we are, not what we do or what we have. If we haven't fully realized this about our happiness, then we will surely realize it as we face death. This becomes paramount in us as we age and are anticipating our life ending. As we grow older, we mellow out about the rat race of life. Much of what was important becomes unimportant. Life is seen more simply, and what we thought were the little things, become the greatest things in life. Do you see the complementary opposite in this?

OUR LIFE HANGS IN THE BALANCE

When we contemplate the possibility of death, we *become* that presence that *knows* what the soul needs to know. Connecting with our Greater Self is the way we can tune in to ourselves and our lives with our mind and spirit fully connected. Centering with meditation or prayerful contemplation allows us to be in a clear and rather divine state, and we are sharper and wiser. Stilling the mind and asking for focus and clarity brings us to a place that knows all that we need to know at the time we need to know it.

Have you ever noticed people who seem to be in a constant state of frenzy? Have you ever been talking to someone who shuffles papers or looks around the room all the while? They are usually type A, workaholics. They are the perfect example of the kind of person who needs to mellow out by resetting their priorities regarding family time, alone time, social time, and work time. If you have an important decision to make, spend some time at home with family or friends, go roller-skating, do some crafts, or some fun activities. This is the advice given to business professionals by many highly educated business consultants.

Another area that we need to balance is the polarities in our perception. When we are faced with a necessary life transition, we have polarities of thought going on from thoughts of the past to worries over the unknown future, and from what is going on in us internally to what is going on all around us that we can't seem to control. However, as we mature or reach midlife, we become a little more subdued and are better able to integrate the past and the future. We are better able to integrate who we are with what we want.

Again and again, plunge into the very thing that makes you afraid so that, in the end, your fear will be eliminated. Think of tackling your fear as a means of conquest and building spiritual and emotional muscle. As you start each day, contemplate your daily plan and visualize yourself going through it, especially when you will be taking on new challenges that worry or frighten you. If you are in balance, with the mind, body, and spirit connected, you can overcome your fears about what threatens you.

We humans are creatures of habit, and when it comes to our fears, we look into the past as a basis on which to see what frightens us. The past doesn't have to control your future. Giving up the past is the key to inner freedom. We must come to a point where we no longer let previous programming rule our lives. Set yourself free to take risks, tackle the unknown, and make it happen for yourself. Any situation that you are involved in can be changed in some way so that it ultimately becomes a successful learning experience.

YOU WILL NEVER GET OUT OF THIS ALIVE

Where does our life energy go when we die? Humankind has been trying to answer this question since the beginning of time. The first law of thermodynamics teaches that energy cannot be created or destroyed. We have a life energy wave level that cannot be destroyed. In that case, it makes sense that death is nothing more than a falling apart or recycling of our Created Self in order that it can be freed to function again in a different, higher order. We are not just things that eventually burn out or break. Returning again to the concept of complementary opposites, death *is* the complementary opposite of life. When we face death, we go from one complementary opposite to the other with the following shifts in thinking.

First, what are the things we think about as we reach the end of our life? Most likely, we think about these things:

- Was I **happy** in love, money, career, health, or fun?
- What did I **want**? Did I get it?

- Was I **good** to my spouse, parents, children, coworkers, and friends?

- Did I make matters worse? We question our **actions**.

- Can I **forgive**? Am I **forgiven**? Am I guilty? Did I let something unspeakable happen?

- Did my life have **meaning**?

Then, if we had it to do over again, what would we do or perceive differently? What would we do differently if we were to have the opportunity to go on living? A new lease on life *finally* puts us into the right gear.

- We change our **values** to a higher level.

- Our day-to-day **priorities** change. We simplify everything and make different choices, especially realizing that changing the exterior is either not possible or not important.

- Our **quality** of life and quality of work alter. We do better on the job, we're more careful, more conscious of detail, we see the big picture and work for that good, and we take better care of our health and everything around us. As we approach the end of our lives, we get pretty wide-eyed in our perception. We even start contemplating the shower nozzle! Every *drop* of life is more important to us.

- Our **attitude** and temperament are better. We are forgiving, accepting of ourselves and others, and we're at peace.

WHAT WOULD THEY SAY ABOUT YOU IF YOU WERE GONE?

Have you read any obituaries lately? Someone sent me a clipping of a person I knew and I was amazed to read a long list of wonderful accomplishments and fine deeds the man had done in his lifetime. He was eighty-four when he passed away. The man was an engineer. Engineering doesn't sound very exciting, but this man had a full life. He designed outstanding mechanical pieces, gave lectures, was an expert witness in complicated court cases, was active in professional societies, was a skier and mountain climber, and he was even an Eagle Scout leader.

How would your obituary read? Not necessarily the public one, although recognizable accomplishments to demonstrate what an individual accomplished and what that person cared about is fine, but how about a personalized summary report on yourself? How would your friends and family speak of you? What would they say about you at your memorial service? Perhaps, from time to time, we should do a personal checkup on ourselves. If we take time to plan our day, our week, our year, and our vacations, why not take time to plan our overall lifestyle and lives? But before you plan your future, you must make an assessment from the past to the present. Put it on paper where you will be more realistic and honest, and then you will be more committed to your personal plan. Otherwise, your personal analysis is just a hazy, fragmented bit of nothingness, subject to change with the slightest breeze.

ENDINGS MAKE BEGINNINGS

Invariably, endings begin with something going wrong. In some cases it is an event, and in other cases it is the ending of a mental state. T. S. Eliot said, "What we call the beginning is often the end. And to make an end is to make a beginning. The end is where we start from." Have I got you thinking? Feeling confused? That's just what happens to us when we go through a transition from an ending to a beginning. When we go through the realization of an ending taking place in our life, we sometimes feel detached, empty, disoriented, disassociated—and a few more *dis* words—disappointed, disenchanted, and disidentified. There is no normal order of reactions to *endings* in our lives.

However, when it comes to dying, Elisabeth Kübler-Ross, who is highly regarded for her work and books on death and dying, states that there are specific stages to the emotions we feel during the process of death or grief. She describes the following stages as sequential: denial, anger, bargaining, depression, and finally, acceptance. This makes sense to me. I've experienced such a sequence when someone close to me passed away. However, other experts, such as Dr. Edwin Shneidman, claim the following reactions are varied based on our needs and drives (including our psychological mechanisms of defense): stoicism, rage, guilt, terror, cringing, fear, surrender, heroism, dependency, ennui, need for control, fight for autonomy and dignity, and denial. All of this depends on our personality and psychological history. Certainly, some people do not accept their death, or for one reason or another, some don't even have the opportunity to find some kind of closure or tie up their loose ends.

When we go through trauma or when loved ones around us go through trauma, we experience little deaths, which change our state of mind one way or another. Dr. Borysenko terms these more significant life-changing traumas as *dark nights of the soul.* She describes crisis as an opportunity for initiation into a life that has more than personal meaning; it is a life that has transpersonal or spiritual meaning. For this reason, it is important to allow whatever string of emotions and thoughts come through us during a crisis in order to process them and ultimately reshape ourselves as improved human beings. We should let ourselves or others go through their own series of reactions to endings.

Whenever we have an ending or little death, we must disengage ourselves. When we choose to disengage, we can feel somewhat empty or disenchanted. This is the time that people can possibly nose-dive into psychological depression, as they long for deeper meaning in their lives. It is advisable to use this nothingness time to *un*learn what isn't helping us, and then learn new things in new ways. Ultimately, at this point we would use our possibility thinking to see new and better paths to take. When we have some trauma or important loss, we may go through a process of questioning the meaning of our life and what we value. Robert Frost refers to this time of disorientation as "lost enough to find yourself." When we experience the dark night of the soul, we have the opportunity to reframe our thinking and make significant changes in our lives. These changes are real, not just changes in positioning ourselves. We change our reality.

When something serious has happened in our lives or we have a close encounter with mortality, many of us make significant career changes, such as cutting down the size of a prospering business just to have more free time, changing from one kind of career to another, moving to a distant location, joining charitable organizations, making religious or spiritual changes, and spending more time with our family and friends.

The reason that most people are afraid to die is that they never really lived. Instead of living and creating the life they want, they try to softly tiptoe through life so that they can arrive at death safely. These are the people who live lives of quiet desperation. Since there is no way you are going to get out of this alive, you might as well live life to the fullest while you are here. In the end, you will not be as sorry for what you did, as for what you *didn't* do but wanted to do all along. Why not direct your life boldly, admirably, and joyously, arriving at death triumphantly? This is the only way to overcome the ultimate impossible situation.

CHAPTER 7

Expansion and Contraction
of Creative Energy

YOUR CREATIVE INTENTION

What You Want to Do with Your Life

Impossible situations in our lives are often created because we are off-purpose. In fact, most people seem to have no idea what their true purpose is. Still, many people seem to know their purpose. We often envy these people because their purpose seems so clear. The truth is that purpose becomes clear when we are ready to live our lives creatively and fully express our Greater Self. Each one of us has a purpose and a chosen life from the moment we are born.

In order to discover our purpose or creative intention, we must believe and trust that a creative intelligence is seeking to create through us. Whatever our field of endeavor, whatever our desires, if we devote our strength to the things we feel suited for and attracted to, something inside us will tell us that it is in keeping with our creative intention. When we feel compelled to do anything in life, no matter how trivial it may be in comparison to the accomplishments of others, this is our true creative intention. This is our calling.

Most impossible situations in life are the result of being off course. We are not fulfilling our creative intention, but instead we are trying to force something to happen that is not in keeping with our life purpose. To create a better world, we must start with ourselves.

We receive our life from the creative intelligence in two elements: the mind and the body. The mind expresses itself through the body as well as moves the body. The two are inseparable. The continuation of human life is impossible with only one of the two.

It is essential to understand that when we unify the mind and the body, our power to overcome the impossible is unlimited. This includes illness, financial problems, and relationships.

The mind and body are not exactly the same, nor are they entirely different. The body is the visible portion of the mind. When we look at a tree, we forget that half the tree is below the ground. Problems begin when we learn to accept as real only what is obvious. The limitations of the body are largely set in the mind.

FOCUSING OUR CREATIVE ENERGY

Each one of us has an energy source where we can focus our power of creativity. This energy source is at our center of balance. Physicists have defined the center of gravity of an object as an infinitely small point on which an entire object can be balanced. This is not just an intellectual concept nor is it merely a physical location in the body, but a dynamically active center of balance and stability. This centeredness or power affects everything in our life. It may be difficult to comprehend intellectually, but you can experience this mind and body integration through focus.

Creative energy that can overcome any impossible situation is capable of infinite expansion and contraction, which can be directed but not contained by the mind. It is not merely a concept but a real force that can be intuitively perceived and mentally directed. Only our imagination limits its potential.

Individuals who perform great feats such as athletes, artists, and various professionals use this creative energy to excel. We can optimize our ability to turn the impossible into the possible by doing the same. This is the way we remove the lead weights of impossibility.

So much of our lives are spent off center. We are not doing what we want to do or what we are created to do, but rather, what we think we should do. When we are focused on what we really want, not what we think we should have or do, the need for outside approval falls away, our vision becomes clear, and clarity is the point of power.

TALENT—YOUR CREATIVE
INSTINCT

We are all born with innate talents and abilities. It may be only a mere hobby or a pastime, or it may be undeveloped from neglect, but everyone is uniquely gifted to do something better than someone else. These talents usually come so easily that they tend to be taken for granted or undervalued. Keep in mind that skills are acquired, whereas talents are inborn. Talent is not something acquired at school or learned on the job. Talents are unique combinations of inborn skills. Like fingerprints, no two people's talents are alike, but they are so much a part of us that they are sometimes hard to recognize. They become apparent when we pursue our goals.

How do you know what talents you possess? Begin by asking yourself what you enjoy. We are inwardly drawn to activities that can make use of our talents, though this may be somewhat vague at first. Because talents are with us from birth, they usually manifest early in our lives. Recent science indicates that brain connections happen at an early age, where the neurons can be observed under high-speed microscopes that actually show the physical movement of these connections occurring in the brains of babies in the womb and throughout infancy. These connections can be stimulated and therefore increased in number by a mother singing repetitive songs and repeating numbers and words.

The fact that the neurons in our brains make their connections primarily in the womb through our early years is why young children can learn multiple languages, yet adults will have more difficulty learning new languages or even changing their accents. Whatever we learned in our early years will enhance certain skills that become an indelible talent. Perhaps boys played with blocks, toy cars, and trucks at such an early age, therefore it made them naturally gravitate toward the mechanics of cars. Later, a teenage boy may be found working under the hood of a car before he can even drive a car. Some children may develop a natural propensity for music long before they can play an instrument because they heard songs more often when they were infants.

Once our key stimulation has affected our brain connections that wired us up for certain skills, we do exceedingly well at everything that is a repetition of that skill or talent that was developed as an infant or in the womb. From our birthday on, we become more and more talented in those specific areas for the rest of our lives. Many of us put our best talents aside and do what everyone else thinks we should do. The talent might get less stimulation, but it never goes away.

Aptitude tests are a way to double-check our natural talents, but people tend to only touch the surface regarding what these tests indicate, and they only tend to take such tests when they are considering a career change. So many people are stuck doing jobs that are not suited for them. They are doing jobs that not only do not connect with their purpose or passion, but they do not even use their best talents. Take for example family businesses, where the children will eventually take over although actually, they are not talented at the business that their parents started. Unfortunately, some children are molded by their parents to enter careers or family businesses that are not in keeping with the child's true purpose or creative intention. This could be a serious mistake that can create a long period, if not a lifetime, of unnecessary impossible situations.

FINDING PURPOSE

Why you do something is more important than how you do it. Purpose is the overall reason for our actions. Goals are the attainment or specific steps along the way. Your goal may be to operate a business, but your purpose is to provide a service to others. Your goal might be to have a five-bedroom house with a family room and a swimming pool, but the purpose of buying the new house is so that your family will be happier with the additional rooms and facilities. The purpose in buying the new home would be for the intangible pleasure and happiness. The goal is to find a house with the specific additions. Often, the greatest happiness lies in finding the highest purpose in your life.

Many people, when asked, will say that all they care about is earning money. If earning money to buy things we enjoy is not our most important purpose in life, then what are we here for? What is our purpose for living? Is it to get more things, or is it to live a dynamic and full life? Purpose is the meaning you attribute to your goals and actions. The meaning we give to all our actions comes from within us when we ask ourselves *why* we want something. Purpose is why we want what we want. The goal is what we want. Purpose is the primary reason, and therefore the motivating factor, in our lives.

Purpose is seen as a mission or an intangible reason behind our actions. This is why corporations not only set goals, they first make a mission statement, which is their statement of purpose. If you do not know what your purpose is, ask yourself, "What is it that I keep thinking about and *why* do I think about it? What have I always wanted to do but haven't done yet, and *why* do I consistently desire it?" It may not even be clear to you yet, but thinking about it will help you bring it to the surface. By defining your purpose, you will have a way to gauge whether you are on track with your life. Unfortunately, we often measure results by material possessions or status in the community or workplace, but these can be aimless goals that may never really be satisfying.

Even if you think you would be happy with certain material possessions or a certain career status, you may not realize how much more happy and fulfilled you would be if you went after your real passion, which is always linked to your purpose. One of the ways to discover if you are on purpose is to ask yourself, "Would I still expend this energy if I didn't have to work for a living? Would I do this, even if I were not getting paid?" If you ask this, over time, you will come to a conclusion about whether your life is on purpose.

Happiness is not tangible. The key to happiness lies in having a purpose that is not just about getting what we want. When people look for higher meaning in their lives, they often gravitate toward the pleasure of doing charitable things, or at least their focus is on giving to their loved ones. People tend to realize later in life that beyond having what we want, the key to true happiness lies in exercising our capacity to give rather than get. If our purpose is beyond the game of having more and getting ahead, we can focus on helping others and find true happiness in the experience. Then we are no longer defining our worth by how much money we have or how to get ahead, but rather on who we are as our greatest self.

CREATING WHAT WE WANT

Before we begin a long trip or a vacation by automobile, we usually check out the automobile to make sure it is in condition to make the trip. We change the oil, check the tires, and tune up the engine. Only when we are sure that everything is functioning correctly do we feel a sense of security that we will have a safe trip.

Life is much the same. As we travel on our journey of life, we must make sure of the ability and strength of the vehicle in which we are traveling. We must check all the parts of ourselves that will make the journey as safe and secure as possible. In short, we must put ourselves in order and make sure we are not leaking strength and ability but have full power to make the journey.

Creatively planning our lives involves making an assessment of where we have been, where we are now, and where we want to be. Asking ourselves the following questions will allow us do a reality check of where we are now and where we want to be.

What

What do I want, what is the goal?
What is the tangible/measurable outcome I want?
What are the obstacles?
What are the intermittent steps/intermittent goals?
What must I give up or change?
What must I do right now to help myself?

Why

Why do I want this (intangible benefits)?
Why do I have a passion for this?
Why does this give me pleasure?

How

How can I accomplish this?
How can I *create* this?
How has anyone else achieved this?
How do I know what steps to take to get what I want?

When

When will I start?
When will I be at each stage?
When will I reach it?

Where

Where will it take me?
Where am I now in relation to where I want to go?
Where do I find my resources?

Who

Who can help me?
Who can teach me?
Who will support me?
Who will I celebrate with?

CREATIVE ENERGY

How do we tap our creative juices to move us toward getting what we want? First we need to tap our creative genius, then we need to focus in the right direction. Scientists have been telling us for years that we only use about 10 percent of our brain. What about the rest? How can we use more of our brains?

Have you heard of right-brain/left-brain interaction? This is how we can use more of our brainpower, by stimulating the use of both sides of our brains. The left side of the brain controls linear thinking such as mathematical ability, logical reasoning, tasks, and movements. The right side of the brain is the creative side, controlling conceptual reasoning, receptivity, feeling, and sensing. Scientists have also said that less than 5 percent of people have the natural automatic tendency to use both sides of their brains interactively. Most people shift back and forth from the linear to the creative sides of their brains, but remain in either side without readily accessing the opposite side and allowing one to interact and influence the other. We have the ability to use our brains more interactively; we just need to use techniques that require us to use both sides of our brain at once.

When we first wake up from sleeping, we tend to be more in the right side of the brain. If we didn't have schedules, we'd start our day more slowly. This is why we may seem to be procrastinating when we are just floating around in the right side of our brain.

A business consultant named Janelle Brittain suggests that people who have difficulty getting in gear can trigger the left side of their brain by working a crossword puzzle at the breakfast table, especially if they set a strict time limit on completing it. Another left-brain exercise for the morning would be to get out your day planner and, as you plan your day, all sorts of facts will pour out of you. But take note, as you use the day planner to unload the linear mental data in your conscious mind, you will free up your conscious mind to let creative ideas come forward as well. If you find yourself getting exhausted mentally, take out some paper and start doodling. You might actually sketch out what your linear mind is trying to sort out. This is the way to integrate the use of your brain. There are numerous techniques that we can use to brainstorm.

When you unload your conscious mind of a bunch of linear data, you free up your mind for creative thinking. If there is too much linear data in the way, it will block your creative flow. Once you empty the overloaded data, you can strike a balance in your right-brain/left-brain thinking.

So many people keep their minds full of facts saying, "Oh, I can remember that," but trying to hold on to lots of information specifically blocks their ability to be innovative. It blocks their ability to bring creative ideas into the conscious mind. Now that we are in the information age, we can use our organizer books and computers to store all that stuff. Give your mind a chance to expand by using all of your brain and letting the dynamics of creative energy expand your horizons.

IMAGINATION CREATES POSSIBILITIES

In our society, imagination is an underdeveloped resource. By setting up a positive image of what we want, our beliefs will facilitate us in getting what we want. Visualization and positive affirmations are the tools, as well as understanding the creative process.

By using visualization to see your goal in a completed manner, you will eliminate or certainly reduce the stress of trying to achieve something you wouldn't ordinarily believe can be yours. Psychologically, if you can accept the end result, you will be able to be more relaxed and creative because you won't be trying to force something to happen. Instead, by imagining it in your mind as something you already have, you can have it almost effortlessly.

Something to remember is, *less* effort creates *more* results. When you are trying too hard to force something to happen, your energy is distorted by too much tension that comes from feeling desperate or perhaps being fearful. This underlying energy is subtly affecting your relationship with people around you, and subtly affecting your resources in an unfavorable and distorted manner.

For example, if you are competitive, you are coming from an ego drive where your focus is on defeating others in order to be first or the best, which is not such a positive concept. Instead, if you are focused on your purpose in alignment with your vision, you are in a very positive state of mind with heightened awareness. This state is what will keep you clear-headed and it well help you to be attuned to valuable opportunities and possibilities.

IMPRINTING WHAT WE VISUALIZE

Visualization or applied imagination is one of the most significant tools we can use for change. It is the process of maintaining a thought long enough so that the mental picture we create evokes an emotional response. The emotion causes conviction, and conviction causes reality. Thus, thought plus emotion creates conviction. Conviction creates reality.

When you focus your mind on the result you want, your brain will facilitate desirable directions and opportunities that will ultimately get you where you want to go. Visualization has a more profound impact on your subconscious mind than you might realize. Your subconscious mind does not distinguish between whether you are imagining something or actually experiencing it. You can make changes in your opinions, beliefs, and levels of expectation by vividly imagining the experiences and circumstances you select.

The only kind of imagery that will alter the subconscious image of reality is *experiential* imagery. Therefore, it is beneficial to create an image that has movement, like a film, not a snapshot. You must clearly identify yourself with the imagery. If you can't see yourself being, doing, or having it, you won't get there. Active visualization, with yourself as the proponent, is a key step in the process of transitioning from a sense of lack to a sense of limitless fulfillment. Visualization can make your life *sensational.*

SELECT AND AFFIRM WHAT YOU WANT

We are constantly creating when we use our imagination, but when this activity is not appropriately selective, we may tend to limit our possibilities by capturing images from our past and creating the same situations in the future. When we desire positive changes, it becomes crucial to practice the imagination of awareness, including ourselves as the proponents of moving, experiential images. To avoid dictating our future out of past limitations, we must actively imagine the future we desire with ourselves as the key player.

Next, we can solidify these images of what we want by affirming them with quality thoughts, which will validate and confirm the images as true for us. The actual process of applying affirmations and imagery is called *imprinting*. Imprinting plants the image we want in our minds as real and believable. Our faith and belief is part of the natural process of creation. When we imprint images of what we want, we reconstruct what we think about our ability to have what we want, free of the barriers of too much caution and overpracticality. When we expand our minds with our belief in creating what we want, we open a gateway to unexplored paths and surprising results.

GATEWAYS TO THE CREATIVE PROCESS

There are various avenues that stimulate the creative process, opening the gateway to creative ideas.

- *Sensitivity to problems:* The ability to recognize what is wrong with things can be our trigger for possibility thinking.

- *Ideational fluency:* This is the ability to rapidly list meaningful words that relate to the overall criteria. For example, someone might be looking for a list of objects that are orange, edible, and crunchy.

- *Expressional fluency:* This is the ability to list related words that express meaning in the relationship.

- *Spontaneous flexibility:* This is the ability to trigger original thought with little or no limitation.

- *Adaptive flexibility:* This is the ability to perceive ways to *adjust* when the original direction of problem solving using spontaneous flexibility is exhausted of ideas.

Each of these expressions is enhanced by an additional factor, which is our unique way of channeling information and ideas in our minds. We each have various learning styles, but some of us have more of one kind than the others. These learning styles are visual, auditory, and feeling (also known as kinesthetic).

Some people have difficulty getting a clear visual picture in their mind. If so, they are likely to be people who hear more or feel more than they actually tend to visualize. The people who are less visual can build into their images the learning style that works best for them, such as auditory or feeling. If this is true for you, just concentrate on the feeling or focus on sounds during your visualization exercises.

EXPANSION AND CONTRACTION OF
CREATIVE ENERGY

If you clearly focus on the result, then all the related *facts* and *ideas* that support the idea will come flowing forth, especially if you write or diagram your thoughts. All forms of energy must be focused and harnessed toward the result you want.

A book by Robert Fritz called *The Path of Least Resistance* describes the creative process as energy that always goes toward what you envision. In other words, if you get a clear picture of where you are right now, your *current reality,* and then focus on what you want, your creative energy will *always* direct you on the *path of least resistance* toward what you want. This is a simple law of nature regarding all energy, and is as sound as the scientific laws of probability.

For example, a river will simply flow around rocks as its energy is directed toward the sea, roads go around mountainous terrain rather than over it on the way to a town, electrical energy rushes through a coiled and tangled power cord to a light bulb, and thus to the path of least resistance. Therefore, if you create a positive tension between your current reality and where you want to be, your life force will do whatever it needs to get you there. The key is to keep your eye on the goal, sending your energy toward what you want.

What we tend to do so often is take our eyes off the goal, in effect, turning our light switch on and off, over and over again. This interrupts the creative process that would automatically guide us on the right path. We tend to lose momentum, like the person who starts a diet during a holiday time of overeating and then wonders why he or she gained weight, gets discouraged, and quits. We need to continue the diet long enough to see the results of not the holiday eating, but of the days of dieting that followed.

Results are forthcoming, but we must keep our *momentum* up, rather than turning on and off the momentum of the creative process. If we have what appears to be a setback, give the energy of the creative process a chance to show you how to *adjust* your course. Robert Fritz refers to this as *create and adjust.*

Applying this concept of the creative process to the methods of innovative thinking where we use right-brain/left-brain thinking, we can use the right side of our brain for scanning creatively through our left-brain database. Next, we can use the left side of our brain to logically sort all the facts to be considered, but we should always remember to check our conclusions and/or ideas with the right side of our brain again to know what is intuitively right or true for us.

By incorporating our intuition and other right-brain senses, we become emotionally motivated by our compelling purpose and passion. This process will happen automatically for us if we give the creative process a chance to work. What generates our creative energy is our application of the right amount of positive stress or tension. We create the right amount of energizing tension when we clearly focus on the difference between our current reality and our vision of what we want. Keep your eye on the goal, and the laws of natural energy will move you automatically on the right path toward your goal.

CONTRACTING RATHER THAN EXPANDING OUR CREATIVITY

As you know, the spiral of impossibility will carry us down into a black hole of failure, which is blatantly a contraction taking us away from any chance for creativity. There are other subtle ways that we avoid exploring our creative potential and avoid taking risks that would have expanded our horizons.

Our own negative thinking, or *stinkin' thinkin'*, as the noted motivational speaker Zig Ziglar often refers to it, includes a whole cadre of subtle ways that we avoid taking the opportunities that could lead us to our success. Our psychological framework could be filled with fear, anger, poor self-image, or feeling controlled. Some of us do something even more subtle to avoid our own success; we make alternative choices without even considering what we are passing up. We don't even notice that we lacked the creative guts to go after our dreams. You know what they say: No guts, no glory.

For example, some people give up the full expansion of their talents by becoming a teacher of that talent without ever pursuing their own advancement and success. They undercut themselves by seeking to fulfill their desires through another while they sit on the sidelines. Then, as their lives slip by, they become jealous, bitter, and cranky about their lost passion. Perhaps out of jealousy some educators will discourage rather than encourage their students to go for it. Thus, we have another generation of folks coming out of academia who have been squashed by the overintellectualized norm.

Others may give up too easily, accepting the message of a rejection letter where their work has been criticized based on one person's opinion. For example, when an author submits a manuscript and it is not only rejected by the publisher, but the respondent writes that the manuscript should be pitched out, an individual could remain creatively blocked for years as a result. For another example, if an actor gets bad reviews on a play that failed, he or she might turn down the next offer for a key role fearing that it is too challenging. In general though, artists expect rejection, but what about people in the workplace where similar kinds of rejections occur? How can we come back around and do more of the same work that just got rejected?

We need to use the creative process to review any feedback, taking the good advice, and discarding any advice that is obviously invalid. After we are clear about our current reality, we need to allow ourselves the chance to feel the emotional impact of the rejection, and then quickly heal our wounds by washing them away. We need to view what occurred as what it was: a temporary injury, not something to be ashamed of. Then we can use any period of disorientation to go within and bring forth the creative process to set a new plan. We can come up with a new creative design of what we would like to do next, based on newly perceived possibilities, thus expanding our circle of possibility.

TURN CONTRACTION INTO EXPANSION

When faced with disappointment and difficulty, we have a choice in life of either expanding or contracting our power. Ultimately, we will choose to expand our power, having the behavioral flexibility to change and do whatever it takes to get what we want. In order to change, we must take action without hesitation when the time is right. Since action leads to the possibility of failure, it is easy to see why so many people stay stuck in impossible situations. Often we choose to contract or depress our creative energy, and we become afraid to take action.

The key to freedom lies in the understanding that there is no way we can fail in the long run, and that the human spirit, or Greater Self, can never fail. The Created Self experiences failure because of faulty perception and actions. The good news is that failure is only permanent if we make it so. We begin to understand that all action, whether we perceive it as failure or not, produces a positive benefit in that we have a greater understanding of ourselves and our actions.

Julia Cameron, a successful filmmaker, refers to her own story in her book, *The Artist's Way: A Spiritual Path to Higher Creativity.* Ms. Cameron's story is a great example of turning what appears to be contraction into expansion. She tells us that *gain* can be disguised as *loss,* and that if artists realized this, they would use any losses as tools to redirect themselves toward their ultimate goals. She had heard for years, including from film director John Cassavetes, "Stop complaining about the lousy curves you get thrown, and stretch, reach for what you *really* want. In order to catch the ball, you have to *want* to catch the ball."

In short, she was repeatedly told by others, "If you want to see your films made, you must first sell yourself as a writer and then if one of your scripts is made, and if that film is a hit, and if the climate warms up a little, then you might get a shot at directing." She listened to this conventional wisdom for a long time, racking up loss after loss, writing script after script.

Finally, after one loss too many, she began to look for the other door, the one she had refused to walk through. She decided to catch the ball. She became an independent filmmaker. Ms. Cameron took matters into her own hands, used her money from writing for *Miami Vice,* and assembled the basic equipment she needed for filmmaking. She went on to succeed at filmmaking and as a film writer, producing endless features, short films, documentaries, docudramas, teleplays, and movies of the week.

Through the process, Ms. Cameron asked herself, why all the "hydra-headed productivity"? She realized it was because she loves movies, loves making them, and did not want her losses to take her down. Lastly, she said, "I learned when hit by loss, to ask the right question —*'What next?'* instead of 'Why me?' " She asked herself, "*How* can I create what I want?"

The choice we make between contraction and expansion is predicated on whether or not our desire to change is based on moving *toward* something we want and love, or *away* from something we fear. What drives you? Fear or love? Have you ever asked yourself this question? Does what you do in life come from your love of what you are doing, or from your fear of losing something you value such as your money, mate, or job?

PERCEPTION INFLUENCES POSSIBILITIES

Take a look at the above drawing. Now, let me ask you a question. What do you see? Do you see a convex line or a concave line? Which is it? Some would argue for either perception. However, the line has two qualities. It is both convex and concave. The two qualities are the same and exist side by side. Like the half glass of water, it is all a matter of perception. Perception limits or increases our ability to use our power to keep ourselves in impossible situations or to change them. Before we can change any situation, we must first change our perception.

Changing our perception requires being open to mind expansion, not being blocked by withdrawing into a rigid and contracted state. At the time we are hit with disappointment, we need to avoid tightening our reins out of fear. Rather, we must open the channels of creativity fully, allowing new input from an expanded circle of possibility. If we get stuck, we need to give ourselves a little nurturing and then head out on a journey for new input. The methods for stimulating the journey are many, including taking a walk, riding a bike, exercising, meditating, diagramming ideas on paper, and working with our dreams.

Exercise is an excellent right-brain/left-brain integrator because we are moving our physical body and at the same time perhaps counting or concentrating with our left brain in some way. Find what works best for you in stimulating your creative genius, which will give you the strength to overcome anything.

FINDING YOUR CHOKE POINT

We've had years of programming telling us that mistakes are punishable, therefore risk taking is unwise. Many parents, friends, business associates, and teachers tell us to stay where *they* see us. Then, as soon as we have difficulty, we tend to allow the beliefs of others to be reinforced by thinking they were right. The next steps we try to take will be taken stiffly, as we contract ourselves in what has now become our own resistance to change. Remember, resistance to change is nothing more than *hardening of the attitudes.* Rather than viewing this as our choke point, we could actually perceive our challenges as the beginning of a golden opportunity for us to break through to success. It is our choice, depending on how we choose to perceive it and use it.

Granted, tough times are initially uncomfortable, but we must strike the right balance of allowing enough emotion to feel the depth of the situation realistically (better termed, our *depth perception*), and yet control that perception of what is going on by realizing there is always something positive in whatever is happening to us. If we do not control our emotions with some clarity, we will reduce the effectiveness of our logical reasoning. On the other hand, we should not linger very long. As Julia Cameron stated in her book, *The Artist's Way*,

"Pain that is not used profitably, quickly solidifies into a leaden heart, which makes *any* [new] action difficult."

Do you want to perceive the point of challenge as your choke point or your *turning point* for a breakthrough to greater opportunity and success? Various business management consultants have likened the breakthrough point of opportunity to a cycle of waves. You can see this in Alvin Toffler's book, *The Third Wave,* in a book by George Land called *Grow or Die,* and these waves also are described by futurist Jeffrey Hallett of The PresentFutures Group (who also coauthored the best-seller, *Thriving on Chaos,* with Jim Naisbitt). Each of these authors describes life's cycles as waves, where just as one wave has its peak, it also must have a valley. We have the opportunity to ride like a surfer, skipping from the top of one wave to another, at just the right moment of opportunity (usually when the peak just begins to descend).

CYCLE OF INTENTION— ATTENTION

Intention Creates Attention

Once you are clear about your intention, the only thing you need to pay attention to and invest in are those things that support your intention. Whatever you give your energy to is what you will have more of. Our intention is our overall purpose.

If you don't have a clear intention, you will invest and pay attention to the input from outside sources. Clear out all the debris in your mind, and clear out all the physical debris around you that could interfere with your creative focus. This includes well-meaning advice from friends, mates, family, TV, newspapers, political and religious authority figures, and advertising. The result is that whatever attention you pay to these sources now becomes your intention. This may be positive or negative, so you must be selective.

However, if we don't have a clear intention of what we want and where we want to go, then others will decide what we will pay attention to. Since we are paying attention to what the outside world draws our attention to, it becomes our intention and we go around in circles. The essential principle in creating successful habit patterns is to choose our intention in every area of our lives. Then our habits will be formed only in those areas.

Let's imagine we have no particular intention on the kind of relationship we want. Since we must be in the circle somewhere, we end up in the attention mode rather than the intention mode. Our focus is forced upon us, based on whatever the outside world determines. Any individual who comes along and can get our attention becomes the focus of our life, or our intention for that relationship.

Now let's say we know the kind of person we want. Our focus automatically narrows considerably. We invest our attention in those individuals who match our intention. We consciously choose the kind of person to invest our intention in. Consciously choosing to be a winner shifts our energy away from undesirable relationships and draws us together with other positive, winning individuals.

The more clear you are on what your intention is, the more power you will have. Winning requires shifting your emphasis from won't power to willpower.

INTENTION VS. METHOD

The simplest motto to live by is, if you will make the decision, your subconscious will make the provision. All that happens in our lives is perfect for us in some way. If we lose sight of this and focus too much on the methods we have been told to believe in, we will limit our subconscious minds from providing us with any innovative solutions.

Oversights can occur when we limit our creativity by our attachment to methodology, just as a multiple choice test limits our choice of answers. Another way we can limit our ideas is by limiting our method of research and the investigation of learning as we hold on to our habitual, logical scheme of perception. Learning theorists have had considerable difficulty doing definitive studies on the concept known as insight.

A creative act is an instance of learning, as it involves trying something new and then producing it by stimulation and response. As the creative process is continuously studied, scientists plan to use tools to assess individuals' creative potential in searching for governmental and industry leaders who have inspiring vision. Science continues to study how creative qualities can be developed by educational procedures. Computers and other mechanical devices are being designed to stimulate human perception, insight, and creativity.

What we know is that the cognitive side of creativity and inventiveness includes two essential elements. One is the process of rethinking and reanalyzing the perceptual field, allowing a shift in *perception*. The second is the appreciation of the new thought by seeing it as an ideal idea. This gives it *attention*—the kind of enlightening attention people describe as a light bulb flashing on in their minds.

In addition to the cognitive side of creativity, there is the motivational and personal side. For example, if during a brainstorming session among colleagues, someone who finds it necessary to do name-dropping for the sake of his or her insecurities clearly has the wrong intention and obviously is thinking of *getting* attention.

Another person has the wrong intention if in such a brainstorming session that person is motivated to steer a solution in a direction that is obviously in his or her own personal favor. This individual may not give credit to someone else in the group for ideas because of his or her desire for personal gain and/or personal recognition (wrong attention). Ultimately, brainstorming sessions would be far more successful at finding solutions if such groups understood the difference between being self-serving (wrong *attention*) and having purposeful *intention*.

INTENTION IS WHY WE CHOOSE OUR DIRECTION

Why we do something is more important than how we do it. The why is our intention and the how is the method. Your method can be creative and innovative, or it can be mundane. All that matters is that you are linked to *why* you intend to create what you want.

Life is a journey. If you wanted to take a trip, you would have to have a reason for the trip. This is your intention. Your choice of transportation would be your method of achieving your intention. Each life intention involves many choices regarding methods. The next thing to consider is whether to take the long route or the short route. Which direction shall we take? Is there a right direction and a wrong direction, or are some just easier than others?

Since intention is so important, we must look at what our true intention is. A clue here is that many intentions are unconscious. In other words, we made a choice earlier in life (based on survival) and even though we say we want one thing, we are actually moving toward another. We may say we want money, but our survival mechanism says we should not take financial risks. We may want a relationship, but our survival mechanism says that we don't want to be hurt. Our true intention may be hidden, yet it is constantly revealed in actions.

DIRECT YOUR SUBCONSCIOUS MIND TO CREATE WHAT YOU WANT

We must have a *reason* for creating what we want, as the subconscious mind is the *prover* and the conscious mind is the *thinker*. In other words, once we know in our conscious mind why we want to create something, then we should run it past our subconscious mind to prove it to be so. The prover proves, and the thinker thinks. Otherwise, if we do not listen to our intuition, which flows from the subconscious, our input will be totally from our exterior environment. The combination of listening to your intuition and then programming what you know to be true is what produces the best possible results in your life.

However, if your subconscious mind is filled with dominant thoughts that are negative memories from the past, you will perpetuate the past in your future. This is why it is critical that you use visualization with affirmations to imprint a new and better future of your choice. Otherwise, you will either resist doing what you need to do to get what you want, or you will re-create failures from your past.

The key to success is to have dominant thought patterns that are totally aligned with what you want instead of what you don't want. If you are thinking about what you don't want, it becomes the dominant thought in your head that drives your brain's neurology. To the extent that you focus on what you don't want, you will create it. If you want money but focus on avoiding poverty, you will unconsciously create poverty. Your dominant thought will cause you to miss possibilities for what you want because you are looking for what you don't want.

VALUES—KEY TO MOTIVATION

Our *reason* for wanting to create anything in our lives must be true to our values, otherwise our intent will be distorted and subject to failure. Our values are our truth, therefore our values are our *proof* that what we want is what we are willing to direct our attention and energy consistently toward.

When it comes to motivation, moderate motivation is best. Too little motivation leads to *aimlessness* and too much motivation reduces flexibility. Values prevent *aimlessness* and drive us at just the right pace toward our goals. We will remain appropriately flexible when we stay focused on our purpose and values in all that we do. When we are clear about our values, we are drawn toward what we want, and we will react strongly to anything that pulls us away from it. Therefore, if you want to know what your true beliefs are, take a look at your actions.

Moving toward values determine what we pay attention to. *Moving away* from values determine what we avoid. You will move toward what you truly want (pleasure) or away from what you don't want (pain or conflict). Values are the key to motivation. Values will allow us to move toward what we may fear when we see that what we value is possible as the end result. Values determine how we spend our time, money, attention, and energy. Put simply, you will end up doing what is important to you and not doing what is not important to you.

Values motivate us to manifest our goals, and goals are the means we use to manifest what we value. Goals create positive pressure. Setting a goal acknowledges to your subconscious mind that where you are is not where you want to be. Values and goals must be aligned. For example, if your goal is to make a lot of money at the races, but you have an opposing value that money is really not that important or that it is wrong to earn money gambling, you will end up a loser simply because you have opposing or conflicting values.

GOALS ARE AIMLESS WITHOUT PURPOSE

Here's how the scenario goes:

Right decision, wrong time.
Wrong decision, right time.
Wrong decision, wrong time.
Right decision, right time.

We can either realize these points after something has gone wrong, when it's too late, or we *consciously* use these points in advance to appropriately weigh our decisions. Expanding your consciousness, as described throughout this book, is the key to making the right choices in alignment with your goals. Your life is a play of consciousness where you are the *creative director* of your own success. We need to understand that we are not controlled by others or controlled by what is exterior to us unless we mistakenly choose to view all that is around us as limiting and controlling.

Knowing that our best answers are within us and that we must make our own choices based on our *attunement* to all there is in the universe empowers us to create our best future. Our attunement to what is exterior, balanced with an attunement to our Greater Self, frees us to make creative choices for the best reasons. When we are out of attunement, our ideas may be distorted and faulty. Then, surely, our faulty ideas will create faulty experiences.

GOALS ARE HOW WE ACHIEVE OUR INTENTION

Our intention is our purpose, which is born within us and which motivates us and gives us the power to create more and more of what we want. If you are unhappy with your present concepts and with your basic philosophies or ideas, look farther, look higher. You will find something *more.* Expanding your consciousness means expanding your ideas and beliefs, and as you do this, you will automatically experience more of the ultimate power, as the greatest source of intelligence and wisdom is in the universe. Universal substance will supply you with those insights that you are prepared to comprehend and effectively apply.

You know the old adage: Seeing is believing. Yet, the opposite is true: *Believing* is seeing. Our clear and firm belief is what triggers our innovative genius into action. It is our commitment to our goals and our belief, through visualization and affirmations, that makes them our reality.

PURPOSE MAKES YOUR GOALS BELIEVABLE

How can our goals be believable if they are not specific? People often say they want a bigger house, more money, a nice place to get away, but how can they believe this when the image of the goal is so unclear and therefore aimless? Surely our minds do not know how to picture what more is. Our minds picture clear images; they aren't hazy. Setting effective goals that can be actualized need clarification by writing them down and making specific choices as to *what* we want. The choices are based on our purpose.

Why have a bigger house? *What* specifically does a bigger house include? When we ask ourselves why (which is our purpose) and what (which is a specific goal), we naturally ask ourselves how to fulfill the goal with a clear purpose, such as the family will be happier (and you can imagine all the reasons why and how they will be happier) if the children each have their own rooms. OK, so exactly how many rooms will the new house you want contain? Once you clarify this, you can put your dream machine into a specific gear with a clear and reasonable intention.

Once you set goals using clarity of purpose, you are automatically motivated and committed to a specific image. It is then that you are ready to work on those goals in your day-to-day life. You are ready for a labor of love. Ideas without *labor* are *stillborn*.

OUR SENSE OF PURPOSE KEEPS US ON TRACK

Goals that are set in alignment with our purpose keep us from being distracted by exterior influences. Instead of creating what we should, we create what we truly want. Our purpose in creating our life is allowing our Greater Self to be in charge. We are the creative director of our own success. Our subconscious mind proves that what our conscious mind wants is right on.

This clarity, this level of being and doing, supersedes all self-doubt, and any *doubters* around us. The subconscious mind is where all the action takes place, as we integrate our right-brain/left-brain reasoning that ultimately gives us the freedom and boldness to manifest what we truly want. Remember, fortune favors the bold.

LET GO AND LET CREATIVE INTELLIGENCE WORK FOR YOU

Once we have our powerful creative purpose in full force and we've set clear and specific goals, we must *release* our attachment to having those results. If we hang on too tightly, we will distort the energy of the creative intelligence that would normally bring all that we need to us. We must let go and be receptive.

Each day, we need to focus on specific images and then ask for all that we need to come to us. Then, as each day progresses, we need to look and listen for messages. The messages will come to us while we observe the play of life—how things play out for us. No matter what comes our way, we need to stop for a moment and look at what is happening—kind of like Native American shamans do. They observe what is happening, and then process it through their mind and spirit. They ask the great spirit what to do, as they feel their own spirit connected to the great spirit.

Awareness of our spirit is within our creative, receptive part of our minds, which is connected to our soul, our truth. From this state of awareness we can see what is happening and adjust our course. Adjusting our course should be as constant as steering a car. We are always adjusting the steering, and certainly, we drive around obstacles.

Being flexible as we calmly take note of what is happening around us, rather than getting upset, is the way to stay in touch with our Greater Self in order to manifest our highest good. If our perception is distorted, we'll only cause new problems. Staying in balance, or remaining centered, is not only a way to prevent problems, it also reinforces the kind of behavior that is characteristic of our Greater Self. Our ultimate purpose in life is to develop that Greater Self through all we do and experience. If this is so, then *how* honorably we respond or behave when a lot is going on around us or while we are doing a lot of work is the most important part of our play of consciousness. If we stay focused on this truth, we will respond most favorably to any situation.

CREATING OUR FUTURE USING SMART GOALS

I believe each one of us has a destiny or purpose. I also believe that we are going to get on with it, one way or the other. The choice is to either struggle and make it difficult or to accomplish it in an easy, stress-free manner. There are two ways in which to accomplish what we want in a stress-free manner. We can have goals that are so clearly thought out that we feel safe and confident in our choices, or we can avoid stress by being melancholy and afraid to do anything too dynamic. Remember, most people who do very efficiently the minimum of what needs to be done at all (having no clear personal goals), are destined to work for someone else who does.

What we have in life is not determined by what we want but by our values and what basic standard we are willing to settle for. If everyone got what they wanted, we would all be healthy, wealthy, and have fulfilling lifestyles and relationships. Unfortunately, most people settle for much less. In racing, you will find that it is just as easy to earn $50,000 as it is to earn $5,000. It doesn't take any more work, it just takes a greater commitment to excellence. The end result depends on your values and the goals you set for yourself. The purpose of SMART goals is to set yourself up so that your neurology is driven in such a way that it is impossible to fail in the long run. **SMART** goals are:

S—Specific

By specific, we mean saying exactly what you want. Saying you want more money is not specific and it is not measurable. Every goal must be specific and measurable. Instead of saying, "I want to earn a lot of money at the track," begin by setting a specific amount each week, month, and season. The important thing about the subconscious mind is that it works on the principle of the least effort. If you are not specific, it will create an end result that expends the least amount of effort.

The subconscious mind interprets everything literally, similar to a computer. If I write a goal, "I will make $5,000," that puts it in the future. If you put it in the future, it always stays in front of you, just out of your reach. Your subconscious mind takes this literally. Instead say, "I now make $5,000." Since your subconscious interprets everything literally, it will act as though the future is now. Remember, your subconscious only responds to specific and definite commands given in the present tense.

M—Modeling

If you want to achieve a specific goal, you have three choices. First, you can try to figure out how to be successful through trial and error. Second, you can observe what losers do, and avoid what they do. Third, you can observe what successful people do, and copy what they do. The latter is called *modeling*. It is the easiest way to achieve any goal and can be implemented through the following process. Find a model, someone who is already getting the results you want. Keep in mind that no matter how difficult something is, there is someone who has already done it, which means you can accomplish the same result. Find out what they are doing. Do the same thing until you get the same results. The ultimate judgment of progress is measurable results in a reasonable amount of time.

A—Action

You won't take action until you are convinced that the reason why you are doing something is worth the price you will have to pay to achieve it. The reason why you do something is more important than how you do it. The how becomes easy once you focus on the why. Forget about how you are going to win at the races and concentrate on the reason you want to win. A strong enough why will supply the information, creative energy, and drive to accomplish any goal.

Write down why not having what you want will be painful, what it will cost you not to achieve your goal, and how not having it will be more painful than the price you will have to pay to get what you want. This will set up your neurology so that your brain will want to move away from your present situation toward your goal.

Write down ten ways you will benefit from having what you want. Link massive pleasure to your new goal. Write down ten reasons why you must take action now. Take immediate action. Remember, trying is not the same as doing. In life, there is no way you can try. You either do something or you don't. Triers are liars. Lead, follow, or get out of the way.

R—Responsibility

Take total responsibility for your results. Remember, 99 percent responsibility does not work.

Notice the results you are getting from your action. If what you are doing is not working, do something else. Keep changing course until you get the result you desire. When obstacles or problems block your success, ask how questions instead of why questions. Spend 20 percent of your time on the problem, and 80 percent on the solution.

T—Timing

Time is our most valuable asset, yet we tend to waste it, kill it, and spend it rather than invest it. We can no more afford to spend *major time* on *minor things* than we can to spend *minor time* on *major things*. As far as our goals are concerned, there are no unreasonable goals, just unreasonable time frames. Be realistic in setting time frames. Remember the answer to the question, How do you eat an elephant? One bite at a time.

CHAPTER 8

Getting More Out of Life

TOTAL LIFE ENERGY—THE ULTIMATE PRICE WE PAY

Turning the impossible into the possible will require an expenditure of energy. Each of us comes to this planet with a limited amount of total life energy. The allotment of time we will have on this earth is equal to our total life energy. This is all we have. Every moment we spend, whether having fun, working, worrying, arguing with our mate, complaining, commuting to and from work, or doing errands, is time we trade for our total *life energy*.

According to the U.S. Bureau of Census, if you are forty-five, you can expect to live thirty-three more years. This is the average total life energy remaining for someone in your age group.

APPROXIMATE TOTAL LIFE ENERGY REMAINING

Age	Years	Days	Hours
20	56.3	20,540	493,525
25	51.6	18,835	452,325
30	46.9	17,118	411,125
35	42.2	15,403	369,925
40	37.6	13,725	329,600
45	33.0	12,045	289,275
50	28.6	10,439	250,710
55	24.4	8,906	213,890
60	20.5	7,483	179,705
65	16.9	6,168	148,145
70	13.6	4,964	119,218
75	10.7	3,905	98,796

If you are age forty-five and you spend half your life, or total life energy, on necessary functions such as eating, sleeping, commuting to and from work, and body maintenance, you have approximately 144,637 hours left to experience the things that really bring happiness and fulfillment to your life.

TRADING YOUR TOTAL LIFE ENERGY

Money is something for which you trade your life energy. Every possession has cost you a part of your total life energy. You have literally traded your total life energy for the dollars you earned to buy the things that you have. This is time that you will never be able to get back. That expensive car, house, those expensive clothes and gadgets, all have been traded for your total life energy. For example, if your car payment is $300 per month and you earn a net income of $10 per hour, this means that you must give thirty hours of your total life energy each month just to pay for the car.

WORKAHOLISM—OVER COMMITMENT TO A FALSE END

Working hard is one thing, but being a workaholic is carrying the concept of commitment to the work ethic too far. Workaholics are compelled by outside forces and motivated by fear and guilt. They are constantly anxious, aggressive, and stressed out, and underneath there is even deeper discord as they actually feel inadequate and suffer from poor self-esteem.

Work is their way to avoid the pressures from the outside with a false exhibition of competence. Often, this facade of competence is coupled with the handicap of being obsessed with perfectionism. Perfectionists are driven by their fear of mistakes. This fear of mistakes is intensified by the perfectionist's fear that others will see any of their slip-ups, or flaws.

Deep inside, workaholics avoid knowing who they really are, and worse yet, they fear letting anyone else know who they are. They spend much of their time and energy battling against not only mistakes, but also against everything they don't want, instead of focusing on what they do want. They spend much of their total life energy viewing others as adversaries to combat or compete against. If they are not the type of workaholic that focuses on combating others, then they are people pleasers, struggling to satisfy everyone else but themselves.

Workaholics are typically not spontaneous, much less creative. Without creativity, they have no dynamics. They replace dynamics with the facade of workaholism. Workaholism is another means by which we misdirect our total life energy.

DO YOU UNCONSCIOUSLY WASTE ENERGY?

We can use up our energy, or we can boost up our energy. It is our own decision to do things with effort or to do things with an attitude of pleasure. This attitude can be present in even the most subtle ways. For example, there is a lady who speed walks every day around my neighborhood, but I notice that she always pounds her feet against the pavement and thrusts her whole body with every step (not with any extra exercise movement, just a hard gait). Her face is always tight, with her eyebrows knitted, and she never smiles or says hello. It seems like she uses a large amount of energy just thinking that she is working so hard during her walking exercise.

After months of this, I saw her doing the walk with another lady companion, who was walking just as fast with an equal amount of physical movement, yet she glided along almost effortlessly by comparison. The second lady seemed to enjoy the exercise and the walk. The difference in attitudes about doing the same exercise was obvious.

Do you ever catch yourself spending more mental energy than you actually need to do certain tasks? Whenever I catch myself getting too intense or involved in something I'm doing, I remind myself to relax and pace myself, because I'm just using up extra energy with no added benefit. Once I catch myself doing this, I notice how much better I feel and also that I am getting the same thing accomplished with less effort. As an added benefit, I will often find that when I slow down and pace myself, I am more receptive to my creative side, which always gives me ideas how to improve on what I am doing.

ENERGY MANAGEMENT

Certain emotions can give us energy, rather than sap energy from us. The energy booster emotions listed below are obviously positive emotions. We have been taught to believe that emotions are always an interference, something to get rid of, but actually having some feeling gives us our zest for life. Negative emotions are the kind that cloud our judgment and drain us of any sense of energy and personal power. The following energy boosters empower us to succeed.

Emotional Rate Sheet

Energy Boosters	Energy Sappers
Enthusiastic	Controlled
Energetic stamina	Used
Creative spirit	Fearful
Resilient	Worried
Dynamic	Indecisive
Serene	Anxious
Motivated by values	Critical, criticized
Goal/priority oriented	Fatigued
Focused intensity	Angry, resentful
	Anxiety, hyperactive
Hopeful	Hopeless
Courageous	Burdened
Gifted	Detached
Engaged	Ineffective
Competent	Helpless
Powerful	

Energy sappers can not only limit positive, creative actions, they can be so draining that they literally cause adverse physical and emotional symptoms to appear. Physically, we can have difficulty sleeping and digesting, have problems with our heart rate, and experience sweating or chronic fatigue. Emotionally, we can have crying episodes, be aggressive, or become emotionally numb. Even the trauma of positive changes can trigger your alarm system to go off.

If our alarm systems are telling us something, then we can turn them around by resolving what set the alarm off, thus switching an energy sapper into an energy booster. For example, anger is a signal that tells us our needs or wants are not being met or that someone or something has violated us (or is not right with us), or that our values and beliefs are being threatened. By resolving the issue at hand, we can eliminate the energy sapper, putting ourselves back to where we want to remain, which is that of the energy booster.

ENVIRONMENTAL ENERGY SAPPERS

Everything we do involves the management of our energy: how we talk, walk, work, play, and relate with others. Relationships are a constant dance of energy. If in a dating scenario someone comes on too strong, the other party automatically pulls back. This is even so regarding the energy that surrounds us as we stand physically before another. Surely, you have noticed how uncomfortable it feels to have someone get in your face. Perhaps you are aware when you stand too close to someone as you face them in a conversation. Everyone has a different comfort zone regarding how close they will let another person stand in front of them. If someone stands too close, the other will step back a bit.

We are an energy field, and being conscious of our energy during our conversations makes us more sensitive to how we come across to others and vice versa. If we would remain in this most aware and conscious state, we would probably make fewer errors in our interpersonal relationships, such as putting our foot in our mouth. As soon as we allow some kind of energy sapper to throw us off balance, we lose such sensitivity and insight. Further, we cut off our ability to make use of our best talents and skills.

Scientists have studied these physiological patterns of our energy ups and downs, calling them *ultradian rhythms*. It is important to normalize these ultradian rhythms. Of course, you also want to do whatever you can to eliminate the cause of the stress, but our bodies have a bit of a time delay in responding to our state of mind.

If we have been upset, even though later on we resolve the problem, our bodies take a while to catch on to our repaired state of mind. Therefore, our best shot at preventing undue physical signs of stress is to quickly get on with shifting our thinking the moment our attitude or feelings go awry.

Other environmental energy sappers can be found in the office, at home, or wherever we go. There can be all sorts of noises that disturb the ultradian rhythms more than we may realize. Even if you think you are good at tuning out noises, your body is still being affected.

When I am visiting with someone, whether socially or for business, if the person is allowing a lot of loud noises around us, I will find a polite way to ask them to turn off the radio, TV, or whatever noisy device is going on, because I know that even if they think they have tuned out the noise, their body—and mine, too—is subtly being thrown off balance while we are together. Sometimes I realize that the person I am visiting may have been distracted by my arrival and does not realize how disturbing the noise is. Maybe the person was watching the television, but for us to converse, this does not fit. I believe both of us would feel much better and we would relate more directly and clearly without some racket in the background.

RESPONSE TO PROBLEMS

When a traumatic problem occurs, we can either perceive it as a challenge that leads us to opportunities, or we can perceive the problem as a dangerous threat. Here's how it works:

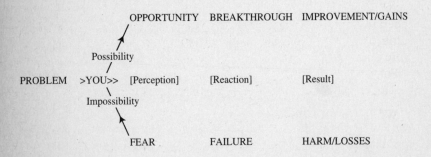

Each time we are faced with a problem, we have two choices. We can perceive the problem as a threat, or we can perceive the problem as an opportunity for a challenge. We can go into distress, or we can feel a positive level of stress—the kind of tension that gives us just the right amount of adrenaline to feel the thrill of overcoming the problem. We block this rush of positive adrenaline if we block the positive energy boosting emotions. Our western culture has pushed us into not feeling emotions, instead, encouraging us to be logical. Using only linear, left-brain thinking eliminates our dynamic sense of challenge, adventure, empowerment, and victory. Some people are so logical that they don't even enjoy a victorious outcome, no matter which road they took to get there.

If we have consumed ourselves with self-doubt, fear, or anger by perceiving problems as threats to our survival, we are just allowing ourselves to be engulfed with feeling that we have no control and that things are happening to us. As soon as we are faced with trouble, we should evaluate our attitude/perception and look to see if we are feeling like a victim. If this is so, immediately turn around the problem by looking for opportunities and challenges.

In these situations, we can shift our focus to the actual current circumstances and review just how unthreatening the situation may actually be. In other words, what is the worst that can happen? What would happen if you took various actions? To test your options, look at what the worst could be and consider the potential gains if you take various actions. Review the possibilities before taking action to give yourself a strong foundation on which to make the most productive decisions.

Are you moving away from your purpose and values or toward them? Expanding your circle of possibility, using your techniques for generative creative insights while adjusting your goals and plans will automatically keep you safe, happy, healthy, and make you wiser and more prosperous on your way to a successful resolution.

For example, a person who is suddenly getting a divorce can review his current situation and see his possibilities as follows:

What Are My Possibilities?

I can be connected in a better way to my former wife.

I can learn new ways to have a loving, successful relationship.

I can recognize what qualities I would like in a new partner.

I can enjoy my time alone and use it as a time to grow and make myself a better partner.

I can review all past relationships and look for patterns to avoid.

I can celebrate the happiness I had from any relationships in my life that were very compatible and successful. (Remember, he can look at various kinds of close relationships, not necessarily romantic ones).

What Is My Personal Challenge?

Challenge	Opportunity
Connect while separated	Discuss comfortable ways to relate with my former wife and kids
Make myself available for for dating	Go places of interest to me where I can meet people to date
Be alone, and not be lonely	Meditate, go on weekly dates with myself, dance at home, enjoy my own spontaneity
Examine myself thoroughly for improvement	Take a seminar on relationships

Actually, the items listed in the opportunity column are only to be viewed as possibilities for consideration; therefore, you can let your mind be more open. You should take a little time to process the options, as you may not be ready to make a commitment to such actions yet. Build your list of options as you consider them and reconsider them.

Next, review them to see how you feel about them through your senses. Take a look at your list before sleeping, exercising, or before you start your day. This way you will be reminded to think ahead, toward what you value, knowing they are challenging and, perhaps, exciting options.

As you go through your day, sleep, or exercise, you will know what sits well with you, but don't let it sit too long or too well, or you won't stretch yourself and take risks or do new things. After all, how do you know what your limits are, unless you've tested them by taking risks that might take you almost too far? If you have checked yourself on the emotional rate sheet, then you can decide that you will risk doing new things, and that these new things really aren't so threatening after all.

After you have laid this strong foundation of emotional security, you will be ready to set some goals, act on them, and make arrangements. It doesn't matter what you can do; what matters is what you will do. With your fears cleared away, you have the will to thrive, not just survive. The stamina you will gain by converting energy sappers into energy boosters will make any habit of resistance dissipate. Your goals will be clear, and you will be effective because you've gotten rid of all the excess fat that carried those toxic energy sappers.

VALUE YOUR LIFE ENERGY—GET RID OF THE FAT

Scientists say our fat holds toxins in our bodies. This is why we have so much more energy when we lose weight. It is not just because we're free of the weight of the fat, it is because we are cleansed of toxins. A low-fat diet is now being touted as a way to live a healthy life. It is important to cut the fat not only from our diet but from our lives.

In your life, fat represents all of those things you think you need to be happy. You will find them everywhere. Most of the fat is the result of the more is better syndrome . . . the belief that inner fulfillment comes from possessions, that emotional discomfort can be alleviated by something external. As a child, satisfaction came from a baby bottle, bicycle, or blue blanket. As an adult, we are often convinced it comes from a bottle of Scotch, a BMW, or a financial security blanket.

Since we will consume a portion of our total life energy for money, we must decide on how that money will be used. There is nothing wrong with having money. The manner in which you earn and spend the money is what really matters here. If you acquired your money doing something you love to do and managed to help others in the process, the expenditure of your total life energy was in proportion to what you received. If you spend more than you earned on things you don't need or try to buy happiness or impress other people, you are in big trouble. You will never reach the fulfillment curve and will remain in the valley of despair.

Most of us equate work with getting paid or having an income. We assume that if we are not getting paid, we must be playing. Sometimes play can look like work, and work can look like play. Have you ever heard someone say, "This job is so much fun I don't feel like I am working?" This is the ultimate test of being on purpose.

However, if money is involved, doesn't this mean we must be working? Generally, if no transaction of money is involved, we consider an activity unnecessary or simply frivolous play. Taken a step further, we usually view any unpaid activity as worth less than a paid activity. There is an almost universal belief that if we are not working for money, building a career, trying to get ahead, we are not fundamentally worthy as people.

To me, money means freedom. Instead of buying things, I use it to buy time. Many years ago I had a wise and wealthy teacher who opened my eyes to the real value of money. He said, "You may have an unlimited amount of money someday, but you will not have an unlimited amount of time. The only way is to buy time to do what you love to do. If you earn money doing what you love to do, you will never work another day in your life and you will have enough money to pay others to do what they excel at."

He said that instead of painting your own house, fixing your own car, and typing your own letters, find people who have achieved excellence in these areas and pay them to do it, and do it well. By achieving excellence in your chosen field or occupation, you will have more than enough money to pay others to do the things you are not good at. This is buying time. You can either use the time to earn more than you would save by not paying them, or you can use the time you would spend on tasks that you were not good at and did not enjoy to do something you are good at and do enjoy.

This concept has always served me well and has become my philosophy when it comes to money. In business, it is important to figure out exactly what you can do that no one else can do. Then hire people to do everything else. Your goal in business should be to do only the things you can't pay others to do. Always be willing to trade money for time.

We are all good at something or can be good at something if we focus our energy on excellence. If we love what we do, we can achieve excellence. Achieving excellence is the key to lifelong prosperity. If you are good at what you do, no matter what the economy, people will always beat a path to your door to hire you or engage your business or service because there are very few people on the planet that are willing to achieve excellence. Truthfully, I can't even program a VCR. I am not good at a lot of things. I have friends who can do many things, including fix their car, paint their house, and repair their TV. The difference is that, in most cases, it's a necessity because they have no money.

I love what I do, and by investing my time and energy, I have been able to achieve a level of excellence that provides me with an income to pay others to do what I can't and don't want to do. The nice part is that when I hire someone who is good at what they do, they also prosper because, not only are they getting paid and earning a living, but they love what they are doing.

MAKING A LIVING WITHOUT WORKING

Someone once told me that their definition of work is anytime you do something but would rather be doing something else. For most people work is just that: doing something we don't want to do to earn money to compensate us for the time spent so that we can do or buy things that will make us happy. To me, happiness is loving what you do and getting someone else to pay you to do it.

When you were a child, you were probably asked, "What do you want to be when you grow up?" What was your answer? Was it something that came from inside of you that you really wanted, or was it something that you felt the adults wanted you to say? Did you select your college or career path because that's what you really wanted to do, or did others choose for you?

An important clue to whether you are happy or unhappy lies in the question, "What do you want to be?" More than likely, your answer was not what you wanted to be, but what you wanted to do. This is the reason so many people are unhappy in their jobs and careers. They have confused doing with being. Our identification is tied into what we do rather than who we are. This is why we introduce ourselves as secretaries, doctors, and computer programmers.

If you are working a job or you are in a relationship with someone or if you are expending any effort in your life and you are not sure of the benefits you will obtain, you will have great difficulty maintaining the necessary enthusiasm, persistence, and dedication. Freud said that "goals cause frustration and anxiety," and he was against the establishment of specific goals. On the other hand, Viktor Frankl said, "We cannot live without goals, because man's basic nature is to be goal-oriented." They were both right. The biggest mistake that people make is aiming too high or accepting too much too soon. Sure, you can have it all, but first you've got to reach some initial goals along the way. You can't be an Olympic ski champion unless you've at least met the most basic goal of learning how to ski.

However, once we set up a sound system for setting realistic goals, then we will find that our dedication and willingness to do whatever it takes will set a great system of cause and effect into play. When this natural, scientific system of cause and effect comes into play, opportunities will present themselves, allowing us to reach goals with less and less effort.

Let's go back to the example of the desires of the person who wants to become a world-champion skier. As he or she focuses on a skiing career, he or she will meet intermittent goals all along the way, and at the same time will create a broader and broader network of contacts and resources. As a result, more and more will come automatically, by word of mouth, to the skier. Thus, what was a challenge before becomes automatic. However, as the skier progresses, he or she sets goals that are constantly stretching the skier further and further. This is the way to grand success, where we must always continue to reach further and continually be willing to work hard as well. In the end, the journey is continually rewarding, as each new and higher goal is achieved. This is the path to greatness.

A lot of what did not come automatically in the beginning comes automatically as we advance. As these opportunities come to us automatically, what also happens is that we attract the opportunities that are sometimes beyond our original expectations. When it comes to skiing, the basic skills are completely automatic to the experienced skier. The same is true of opportunities. What was a challenge to research and gather as a resource before becomes automatic to the skier who has been working at a skiing career, and more and more grand opportunities appear.

We hear stories all the time of people who are discovered or receive an incredible opportunity that takes them a quantum leap farther than they had even hoped for. This is the dynamic of winners.

This winning dynamic works for them. Losers are too busy complaining or plodding along to be capable of opening their doors for quantum-leap opportunities.

Through it all, the skier is in his or her element day in and day out. He or she is in the rapture of passion on a daily basis. Therefore, every practice session, even when filled with challenges, is a pleasure. As the skier advances, backers and financial rewards appear. Although you might think that skiing is more exciting than other careers, some people are turned on just by feeling the pleasure of working with people. This kind of quantum-leap dynamic is true in any career when people align their career choice with what gives them a charge.

When some people are asked what their talents and skills are, they are not so good at answering the question. Why would they not know the answer instantly? Perhaps it is because they have not taken the time to objectively review what they're good at and why they do what they do. We should clearly know what our talents and skills are and match them to our career and our overall life plans. We can identify those skills by looking at how we felt when we accomplished certain achievements in the past. Was it meaningful? Did you have a great desire to do it at the time? Would you do it over again if you had the chance?

YOUR PASSION—WHY YOU DO WHAT YOU DO

What motivates you to go to work every day? Is it survival, security, tradition, prestige, power, or success? Is it creativity and fulfillment? The real problem we face is that we are trading our total life energy every single day. There is nothing in your life more valuable than the time you have left. You cannot put too much attention and importance on the way you invest those moments. Start tracking your life energy. How much are you trading it for right now? Write down the actual cost in time and money to maintain your lifestyle.

Two factors occur when you are doing what you love. One, you are motivated because you are fulfilling your passion, and two, because your work is a pleasure, it seems like you are making a living without working. Your passion for your work inspires your motivation, making the terms *task* or *work* seemingly disappear from your vocabulary.

Rather than allowing ourselves to be motivated by fear, deficiency, and other exterior influences, we can automatically be motivated by the inner drive of our passion, which makes everything we do seem effortless. When our passion is being fulfilled, we put our heart into our work. When we've got our heart in it, we are not driven by exterior commitments, we are driven by our own dedication to what we love. This dedication is an essential inner commitment. It is being true to yourself. Being true to ourselves is characteristic of winners because it generates action. Losers make exterior commitments in the form of promises, which have no real commitment to action.

One way to reinforce your inner commitment would be to tell others, or at least one person, about your commitment to certain goals. This is a strategy that strengthens your commitment to yourself by making it not so easy to get off the hook. First, though, the commitment must exist within you.

The goal of every individual should be excellence, not perfection. Dean Simonton, the author of *Genius, Creativity and Leadership,* indicates that mistakes are a normal part of the process of the geniuses that create excellence: "Great geniuses make tons of mistakes. They generate lots of ideas and they accept being wrong. They have a kind of internal fortress that allows them to fail and just keep going."

Notice the following winning formula:

$$Ability \times Effort = Results$$

Further note that it does not say

$$Ability \times Perfection = Results$$

It says *effort.* Also note that ability is having the smarts not to waste effort.

Trying out new methods and stretching ourselves beyond whatever our previous limits were opens the door for the dynamics of innovative genius. Little failures, like little deaths, tell us when to change direction. What doesn't work leads us to new ideas and gives us the opportunity to try them. In the end, we'll find the better way. Thus, we will be more effective in the long run, and we'll be even more effective every time we use our more effective discovery over and over again.

USING ADVERSITY AS AN ENERGY BOOSTER

Adversity can be turned around, not only by using it as a message guiding us in changing or adjusting our course, it can provide us with enhanced focus and energy. The corporate genius, Lee Iacocca, described how he turned his anguish over being dismissed from the Ford Motor Company into an energizing force, propelling him to move on with his rage. He changed his way of perceiving adversity by learning how to redirect his anger, which gave him a new reality. Iacocca wrote in his autobiography:

> There are times in everyone's life when something constructive is born out of adversity. There are times when things seem so bad out of adversity. There are times when things seem so bad that you've got to grasp your fate by the shoulders and shake it. I'm convinced it was that morning at the warehouse that pushed me to take on the presidency of Chrysler only a couple of weeks later. . . . In times of stress and adversity, it's always best to keep busy, to plow your anger and your energy into something quite positive.

In a sense, what Iacocca did was strategically put on rose-colored glasses, at the right time during his recovery process upon being dismissed from Ford.

An issue of *Psychology Today* described seeing "blue skies" as a valuable form of denial when we use it to shift our thinking into a positive mode in order to recover from trauma. The cover of the magazine pictured a guy wearing sunglasses that had blue skies superimposed in the lenses.

When I noted above that Iacocca put on rose-colored glasses at just the right time, I must emphasize that it is important to consciously decide to put the glasses on after we have realistically perceived what is going on. Otherwise, if we deny reality too much or at an inappropriate time, we could make horrendous decisions that could be costly to us. Remember, viewing our current reality is also essential. Then make new choices based on clear and positive possibilities. Then put on the rosy glasses, and go for it. Keep this in mind: If one person has done it, you can do it, too. If no one has done it, you can be the first.

SEVEN WAYS TO BOOST YOUR ENERGY AND MAKE YOUR LIFE WORK FOR YOU

1. *Focus on your purpose and goals.* Focus your creative flow with a passion in the direction of what you value, your purpose and goals.

2. *Know that you deserve what you want.* Respect yourself enough to believe you deserve to have what you want.

3. *Be true to yourself.* Be committed from within. Be who you are, and become what you were meant to be. Do not become what others think you should become. Being true to yourself also means being honest with yourself and others. Be honest with yourself regarding your assessment of your current reality. You can't know how you are going to get somewhere if you don't know where you are.

4. *See the possibilities.* Do not waste your time with energy sappers. Convert your perception and turn obstacles into opportunities. Believe in yourself as a winner who perceives every circumstance as a possibility.

5. *Continuously build your support base of people and resources.* Since things can change at any moment, always keep building your contacts and resources. Have a constant flow of people, information, and ideas available to you. Never, ever think, "Nobody knows," or "Nobody has any."

6. *Believe that you are the creative director of your life.* This should be your most dominant thought. See an answer in every problem. Believe in your own luck. You are responsible for creating your own success.

7. *Just do it.* Don't procrastinate. We have all learned the law of inertia: a body at rest tends to stay at rest, and a body in motion tends to stay in motion. All successful individuals know that

accomplishment is the result of activity. Even the smallest action can eventually multiply into a driving force. There never was a better time for you than this moment. Now is the time for you to take bold steps, knowing you have clear plans and that you are the creative director of your own life. This includes doing new things and taking risks. There is no way you can attain your greatest potential without reaching. Mistakes are OK. It's OK to be wrong. It's OK to lose a bit once in a while. You'll live. Use the checkpoints for focusing your total life energy listed below to organize your plans. Know that your plans are realistic, measurable, achievable, and believable by clarifying and organizing your plans for achieving your goals.

THIRTEEN CHECKPOINTS FOR FOCUSING YOUR TOTAL LIFE ENERGY

1. *Purpose:* Align with goals to create a driving force.

2. *Goals:* Make goals measurable, tangible, specific, and clear.

3. *Dream goal:* Set an expanded version of your goal, allowing for more success. An organizer system called the Personal Resources System refers to these as *gleams.* For example, your goal might be to earn $30,000 on a project, and your gleam might be to earn $40,000.

4. *Investment:* Identify tasks, obstacles, and costs.

5. *Resources:* Make use of money, people, services, associations, etc.

6. *Skills:* Match your talent and trained skills to your goals; otherwise develop them with further education.

7. *Action plan:* Establish how you will create your goal, therefore setting intermittent goals that can be acted upon on a daily basis.

8. *Visualize:* Make it believable. Animate it, which gives it energy.

9. *Affirm* your commitment.

10. *Organize* and plan every day; monitor progress.

11. *Flexibility:* Creatively adjust your course.

12. *Persist* because it builds momentum.

13. *Enjoy the result:* Plan and visualize how you will enjoy the benefits of reaching your goal.

CHAPTER 9

Possible and Impossible Relationships

All the possible and impossible situations in life are profoundly influenced by the relationships we have with ourselves and others. We get an operating manual with things like computers and cars, but we get no operating manual when it comes to relationships. This can be a tremendous drawback since just about everything we do involves other people.

Our ability to interface well with others is probably the greatest thing we can master in life. Not only is it important regarding how we interface, but how we connect or bond with others emotionally. The human connection can limit us, motivate us, control us, or influence our choices because of the emotional or psychological nature of the relationship.

There are many different types of relationships including friends, family, lovers, social, business, coworkers, and, more importantly, ourselves that contribute in a unique way to our ability to turn the impossible into the possible.

We can either let relationships get in our way, or we can let them take us right to the top. Relationships influence our success or our lack of success. Successful people make it a point to associate with other successful people, which helps them to become more successful. Unsuccessful people do the same thing, only they associate with other unsuccessful people. This perpetuates their own game of impossibility, whether they are aware of it or not.

RELATIONSHIPS ARE EVERLASTING

We can be certain of the fact that relationships never end. The *form* changes, but the relationship remains forever. No matter how angry, hurt, or separated we feel from someone we have had a relationship with, the human spirit or shared oneness goes on forever. Death changes but never ends these relationships.

Because our Greater Self is a part of the infinite oneness or creative intelligence, we always have a relationship with everyone. We are related, whether we are aware of it or not. When we get into a relationship, all we are doing is acknowledging this connection. The relationship then takes on a certain form.

In reality, we can never begin or end a relationship with anyone; we can only acknowledge or change the form. When we break up, we are actually changing the form of the relationship from friend to enemy or former friend, mate to ex-mate, partner to ex-partner. This does not change the fact that we are still related and will be forever. Even death cannot end our relationship. It only changes the form.

COMMON RELATIONSHIPS THAT INFLUENCE OUR LIVES

Let's take a look at the most common types of relationships.

- Spiritual
- Yourself
- Friendship
- Romantic
- Parent-child
- Family members
- Business
- Casual

Your Spiritual Relationship

First and foremost there is your spiritual relationship. This is the relationship you have with the oneness, God, the universe, or the intelligence that created it. The focus of religion has been to teach us the best or only path that God wants us to take. Each religion is convinced there is a different path; therefore, I submit that they are all right. There is no right or only path. What is more important than a single path is our relationship with the oneness. If we understand that we are one with it and are here to express ourselves as cocreators to make a better world, there is no way we can be separated from the source, no matter which path we take. We are all on the same trip and will get to the same destination. Instead of focusing on the destination, perhaps we should focus on the trip. The journey is our true spiritual relationship, not the destination.

Your Relationship with Yourself

The second most important relationship is the one you have with yourself. This is formed by what you say to yourself and what you think about yourself. The dialogue you carry on with yourself affirms your innermost beliefs and translates into vivid images in your subconscious. It inevitably influences outward actions in daily dealings in the world. Negative self-talk tends to be circular, nonproductive, hinders problem solving, and is a prime means of harboring hopelessness and impossible situations. Images that comprise our self-talk continuously color our present, even in ways of which we are unaware.

A conscious choice for positive inner dialogue has equal power when manifested in our lives and produces opposite, desirable results. Luckily for us, positive self-talk is also habit-forming and, when specifically directed, is a great strength in our quest for positive change in our lives. Of course, the change starts within, and what better place to address negativity than in our own head and heart.

The hallmark of our relationship with ourselves should be gentle consideration. Too often we utilize nagging criticism or even harsh condemnation to force positive change. In our self-relationship, the means to achieve a certain end must be honest, ethical, and appropriate to ensure true inner growth. When we can afford this level of consideration and dignity for ourselves, then we automatically extend the same courtesy to others. This is also the action behind loving ourselves and allowing joyful expression without fear of inner reprisals. The soul expands under the open guidance of a kind teacher and withers under the negative expectations of a critical watchdog.

In learning to realign our relationship with ourselves, we must practice patience and discipline in equal measure: patience as we retrace our steps as many times as necessary and discipline to be sure we don't give up in premature defeat over the difficult passage of destructive patterns and habits. The work of inner honesty can be frustrating and tiring as we delve through layers of protective deception. However, gentle honesty is the fundamental ingredient in a relationship having a foundation of trust.

Do you feel authentically you, or has your life become an exercise in deceit? Do you have a complete understanding of your true nature, or have you produced a smoke screen behind which you hide, even from yourself? When we allow our inner self to separate in distrust from our conscious self, then our life becomes a shadow act of something that has the potential for authenticity and original creation. In many ways, honesty in our self-relationship is the opposite of fear, since the degree to which we can honestly assess ourselves is inversely proportional to the amount of fear the thought of doing this induces in us.

Honesty in our self-relationship is crucial, but so is trust. Essentially, we must trust ourselves to be an accurate authority on our own life. Taking on this essential role is the first huge step in gaining emotional responsibility. As we allow others to be experts on our lives for us, we abdicate a certain amount of blame for mishaps, but we also relinquish some happiness and pride in achievements. No matter how willingly we allow or manipulate others to bear our rightful load, this always carries a price of some resentment toward those who oblige us as well as a sense of inner disappointment at not directing our own cause. At the Greater Self level, we are perfectly equipped to identify our true goals defined by us and for us alone. We have neither the right nor the desire to release this responsibility into others' hands. As we increasingly take on the business of an honest, loving, inner assessment, we become free in the only true sense. It seems like a dichotomy in some ways, but the truth is that we must take on full personal responsibility in order to be free. Accepting this responsibility without reservation creates the possibility of an expansive expression that comes along with a life lived freely and honestly.

In the middle of this daunting proposal to alter your self-relationship, it can be of help to remember earlier discussions regarding the nature of the Greater Self. The Created Self, which may well be layer upon layer of deception, is merely a flimsy cover obscuring the Greater Self within. This greater or higher self is changeless and unaltered by external achievements, worries and concerns, and collection of material goods. The real you is hidden. The greatest understanding you can have, if you want to be enlightened, is that no one will ever understand you.

The relationship you have with others will mirror the relationship you have with yourself. If you can't forgive yourself, you will not be able to forgive others. If you are impatient with yourself, you will be impatient with others. If you blame yourself and establish unreasonable expectations, you will do the same to others. Does a difference exist in how you treat yourself and how you treat others? What if you talked to others the way you talked to yourself? What if you were as unforgiving to others as you are to yourself? Chances are no one would accept the kind of abuse you give to yourself. If our treatment of others is very different from the way we treat ourselves, this false base can never lead to a whole relationship built on trust. A discrepancy between our treatment of ourselves and others will eventually show itself in an inability to truly connect, or a vague sense of unease. It is impossible to build strong, healthy bonds on a false base and precludes your own faith in your integrity.

Friendships—From Casual to Deep

Cicero described a friend as a second self. How extensive is your circle of friends and acquaintances? How extensive do you want it to be? Are they enriching friendships? Do you have a lot in common? Do you contribute your fair share in nurturing the relationship? Friendships are no casual thing. Once you move past the acquaintance stage, they take some effort and nurturing, or else they just dry up.

No one wants to feel used, and as soon as we figure out that someone is looking to take advantage of us, we retreat. Taking is not what friendship is about. Having a wide range of what we call friends that we would invite to a party is really just the crowd we hang out with. Our close friendships, which have depth, involve an equal share of each giving the other uplifting enrichment and caring enough to talk about the challenges we face.

If you can't talk about what you are going through, then I would question the depth of the friendship. If a friend is unwilling to think positively with you about problem solving, that person really is not a friend but just an acquaintance. Of course, if we were to be in the mode of an impossibility thinker, then sharing our problems will turn our friends off. The give and take of sharing with close friends is an important balance that needs to be worked on, nurtured, and mutually understood. When we are geared toward possibility thinking, we will not find ourselves in the position of appearing to be just dumping, because the friends we talk to will see that we are positive about resolving anything that comes our way. If you fall into a victim trap, you could lose friends, but if they didn't give you a chance to correct this by telling you they are bothered by this first, then they are no friend at all.

Friends can find the right blend that works for them to comfortably share the reality of life. I have a friend who is very tight-lipped and uncomfortable talking about himself, but he can still tell me that he has been going through a lot of "learning experiences," and our way of conversing on the surface still works to lift whatever he is going through to a humorous level that he enjoys. We laugh and joke about life's problems and come out feeling pretty upbeat about all that we deal with from day to day.

Friends are people we enjoy being with because we feel good when we are around them. We like to do things with them, *but what we do is not as important as how we feel* when we are around them. Whether we realize it or not, we form all personal relationships based on how others make us feel about ourselves when we are around them. When people make us feel accepted, appreciated, loved, competent, or successful, we consider them friends. They help us to see the possibilities within ourselves because they are nonjudgmental supporters. Often, they point out what is right about us instead of what is wrong. In a nonjudgmental way, they can even tell us what we are doing that may be endangering our emotional, psychological, and physical well-being. They help to guide us without controlling us. These are the best possible friends. We can love our friends, but the love we express is not the same as romantic love.

Romantic Relationships

Romantic relationships incorporate a deep and profound aspect of physical attraction and desire. Our desire to be with the other person and our loneliness without him or her often causes us to exhibit all the typical symptoms of a good country-and-western song. Nearly every TV show, novel, movie, and song emphasizes some aspect of romantic love. Unfortunately, unconditional love and romantic love are not always the same. Romantic love can be only sexual. Many people fall in love as an excuse to have sex. This frees them from having to deal with the guilt of having sex just for the sake of enjoyment. If I love someone, sex is OK. If I don't love them, I am just promiscuous.

Romantic love can also be combined with a feeling of unconditional love for the person just for being who they are. It is possible to have love without sex and sex without love. The ideal combination in a romantic relationship is to have both with the same person. Sometimes this is not always possible. We have to decide for ourselves what we truly want out of the relationship. Is friendship more important, not as important, or equally as important as having romance or a sexual relationship? An exciting romantic and love relationship will profoundly influence our creativity, our self-esteem, and our circle of possibility.

There are clearly differences in male and female communication style, thought processes, interests, and many times even goals. However, a current trend seems to be couples working together in their own entrepreneurial enterprises. When couples harmonize in their career efforts, they can have a long-lasting and more enriching relationship, but many couples fall apart by finding that their opposites are *not* complementary.

Relationships change dramatically as soon as we *live* with our partner, whether it is at home, at work, or even while just traveling together. It seems that our true colors come to life in full panavision when we get intimately close to someone and that person becomes a family member. All of our family baggage from our development years comes to haunt us unless we do something to prevent it.

When things are out of kilter at home or if you're not living with your love relationship, then you can face each day with discord. A troubled relationship at home can automatically give you negative messages that are the opposite of any positive affirmations you would make. This discord at home can be pivotal regarding our ability to withstand outside pressures.

Instead, we need to enlist our love partner as a partner in the foundation of our life. It can give us strength, but only if we are willing to properly nourish it; otherwise it will die like a plant in need of water. The soil takes your seed, not your need. If you don't plant your garden in the spring, you will be as barren as the desert by summer. Relationships are a nurturing process that help us grow and expand to full maturation.

If we believe that when two people come together they should fulfill each other's personal and emotional needs, we fall into the trap that says, "You take care of me, and I'll take care of you." Instead it should be, "I will take care of me for you, if you will take care of you for me."

Common-Goal Relationships

The common-goal relationship is the most powerful. When combined with friendship, love, and romance, it can be the most dynamic relationship. In a common-goal relationship, we are not only attracted to the other person but are mutually attracted to a common goal or goals. Our energy sphere is combined with the other person's to create a dynamic source of power. The common goal may be children, a family business, service to your fellow man, or sharing the same spiritual practice. Whatever the goal, if we join with another, all the areas of possibility increase twofold or exponentially. The results can be greater than we can possibly imagine.

What I have learned is that mutual goals and interests to which both can passionately commit are the most powerful driving forces within a possibility relationship. The journey becomes more important than the destination. Common-goal relationships assist in transcending individual limitations and agendas and draw from the resources of both partners to achieve a successful, dynamic, and passionate relationship.

Business Relationships

Corporations continually agree that their most important resource is their human resources. When it comes to human qualities or lack thereof, business enemy number one is *inflexibility.* Being flexible is having a sense of *foresight* rather than *hindsight.* Inflexible people are the scoffers who are left in the dust when a team is able to find the means to move on without them and succeed. If the inflexible ones have control, they will take everybody down with them when they should make changes and refuse to do so.

Business managers do not have to exert their authority like a bulldozer crashing down on people. Sooner or later, these individuals will be reading the want ads after their tyrannical style is discovered within the organization. Managers must earn credibility. Therefore, the effective individual does not exert authority but gains acceptance by acclamation.

Management style can make or break an enterprise. We need to be flexible regarding facts and decisions as well as flexible with people. Have you noticed that nearly all business training courses are on the subject of communication in one form or another? All nontechnical training programs are about the interaction of people, covering areas such as leadership skills, interpersonal skills, team building, customer service, and conflict resolution.

Since people can make or break a business, they are the most important factor in the workplace, and their selection is critical. Human resources/personnel departments are geared to assess human characteristics and qualities and consider them to be as important as job-specific capabilities.

When it comes to partnerships or teams, it is important to have a blend of personality styles and thinking styles. For example, a small business that is opening up needs a good bean counter (this term is meant as a compliment to all you accountants and CPAs), a good operations and/or production manager, and someone with finely tuned people skills who can bring the business to the marketplace. If you have two of the same type of person, you only have double the manpower. It would be better to have two people with complementary opposite skills and interpersonal styles so they can multiply their manpower.

There are three kinds of producers: starters, continuers, and stoppers. The starters are the pioneers, the continuers are the implementers, and the stoppers can recognize any pitfalls to avoid. Two starters who go into business are going to have problems pulling it off.

When looking for a job, starting a business, or hiring employees, we need to go beyond the usual kind of interview questions that deal with qualifications and consider the important traits of a person's character. This has been the intention of contacting references, but many times only facts are confirmed, not getting to know what a person is like to work with.

Recruiting firms will go to great lengths to find resources for not only talented people, but people who have the best characteristics that will fit with their organization. If you are part of an organization looking for staff or you are looking for an organization to join, there are places to go where you can find out about people who are polishing their knowledge and interpersonal style, such as professional associations, business groups like the Chamber of Commerce, Toastmasters, or service clubs like the Rotary or Kiwanis clubs.

Mentor Relationships

You can consciously attract people who might make a good mentor for you by directly choosing to attend certain meetings and associations of the skill that interests you. Unconsciously we can attract just the right person at just the right time using our desire and intuition. They say, "When the student is ready, the teacher will appear."

If you want to polish up your interpersonal skills, take some classes, read some books, and especially, join Toastmasters International where you'll enhance your ability to talk on your feet. Toastmasters will give you the opportunity to change your perceptions about yourself and how you view others. Join some groups that stretch who you are. Don't join an easy crowd, because you won't grow. Go where the expectations and the demands to perform are high. Roger Gentis said, "Choose your mentors carefully! People who are lost in their lives tend to follow people who are lost in their theories."

Family Relationships

Family relationships can range from closeness to downright abuse. One of the most popular terms used by popular psychologists and talk show hosts is the *dysfunctional* family. Loosely, the term implies that any family unit that does not measure up to a standard of perfection bordering on *Ozzie and Harriet* or *Leave It to Beaver* is psychologically damaging to our development. It seems like every social ill from rudeness to murder has its root cause in the dysfunctional family.

While it is true that our family backgrounds profoundly influence our development and our ability to create possibilities, we can not and should not use it as an excuse for remaining in impossible situations. Many so-called children of dysfunctional families have overcome their childhood experiences and have gone on to lead very successful lives. On the other hand, many children of perfectly normal families are sitting in prisons.

As with everything in life, it is not what happens to us that matters, but what we do with what happens to us. Also, it is obvious that each person we encounter is coming from a completely different family background. Sometimes the relationships we have with others are a replay of our family relationship. Friends, lovers, and coworkers are just substitutes for the family members we had difficulties with. If we did not resolve our family relationship, there is a good chance we will keep repeating the same behavioral patterns in subsequent relationships.

We all have to work through our family relationships. In the meantime, what is more important is how we feel about ourselves right now and what we are willing to do to turn our impossible situations of the past into possible opportunities in the present.

IMPOSSIBLE OR POSSIBLE DIFFERENCES

How quickly we can switch from harmony to anger with the ones we love and care about. One minute someone can be our friend and the next minute they can be our foe.

Perception is held in the moment; the mind doesn't get a chance to go through much logical processing when we are upset. As soon as someone triggers our emotional buttons, we jump into the survival mode and react by habit. Once we have jumped to a conclusion, we are hard-pressed to change it. If we have been in disagreement with someone and it threatens our sense of being a protected self, we're instantly in opposition. The concept of seeing another as a complementary opposite is out the window.

How can we change this? Perhaps we can change it in three ways. First, by continually working on getting rid of all that negative baggage that has built up inside us, replacing it with possibility thinking and positive vision, second, by investigating our behavioral habit patterns and learning new ways to perceive what we believe is being communicated and practicing new responses, thus forming new and better patterns of response, and third, by giving people the benefit of the doubt by being open and forgiving in understanding each other's communications, knowing that their intention is what counts.

So often we think a relationship is not repairable. With some, it may be time to let go and move on, but many times we leave relationships behind that could be repaired if both parties understood more about where people are coming from.

Too often we want *justice . . . just for us.* Due to our reactionary survival tendencies and the fact that we tend to limit our perception due to our emotions from past experiences, we stay fixed on a "my way or no way" kind of thinking. It's sad that people would rather be right than happy. They cannot accept the unique view of another, they cannot imagine being able to negotiate differences into a win/win situation. Most people do not appreciate the true individuality of others once they start seeing the negative in someone. The fact that we are all so different is what makes life interesting, yet we may not give some relationships a chance by simply asking someone else to treat us or respond to us in a different way. We get treated in life the way we *train* people to treat us.

We need differences because they stimulate understanding and learning from different points of view. If we were all the same, there would be no need to have relationships. A timely quote from my *THINK* book is, "If two people always agree, one of them is unnecessary." Each one of us has something original to contribute in every relationship. Sometimes we focus on these differences as if they were negative, and we miss their value, rather than looking past the differences and discovering the benefits.

Often differences are the force that attracts two people. Opposites do attract. Many times, the same differences that attract cause a relationship to end. In the beginning, we appreciate the differences, but eventually we try to change the other person to be more like us. The very thing that attracted that person to us now turns us in the other direction. Instead of appreciating the difference, we see the difference as a deficiency. If you want to make an enemy, try to change someone.

NONACCEPTANCE OF DIFFERENCES

Impossible or unworkable relationships are often the result of not accepting each other's differences. Unfulfilled expectations often become the culprit that eventually erodes the relationship. From an accountability standpoint, we frequently do not make our wants, needs, and expectations clear to our partner but still get angry when our unspoken desires are not fulfilled. We expect our partner to read our mind and if he or she can't or won't, we often punish our partner through complaining, blaming, withdrawing, attacking, or worse, withholding love. When we truly love someone unconditionally, we do not use emotional blackmail to get what we want.

Examine your most important relationship. Is your love, trust, and acceptance conditional or unconditional? Is it "I will love and accept you when and if you behave this way" or is it "I love you, period." The more conditions we have for love, the wider the gap between us and our partner. Often, we set up a series of conditions that must be met by our partner to satisfy us in order for that person to prove that he or she really loves us. If by chance our partner satisfies these conditions, do we finally let him or her off the hook, or do we increase the demands until they become impossible to fulfill? More than likely, we keep upping the ante until there is no possible way our partner or friend can meet our demands. And again, we get to be right, but we don't have what we want.

There are very few unselfish relationships. When we look at any relationship, we will see that we are in it for a reason. Something is exchanged for something else. There is nothing wrong with that as long as the goal is mutual exchange and not exploitation. When we approach our relationship from a selfish stance rather than a benovelent one, we set ourselves up for an impossible relationship. Instead of deciding what we can bring to the relationship to make it possible, we decide what we want to take from the relationship. If our goal is to get fulfillment from our partner, ultimately we will exploit all our partner has to give until there is nothing left. Even if we're not into a relationship to get, often we still view the relationship as a matter of quid pro quo. If I give something, I expect something in return. This converts the giving aspect of a relationship into a series of loans and debts.

VALUING YOUR PARTNER

We have all heard that familiarity breeds contempt. Unfortunately, this is true. The closer we are to someone, the more lax we become in our communication and behavior. Behaviors that we accept in others are unacceptable in our partner. We set tougher standards for our mate and expect more of him or her because after all, if our partner truly loved us, he or she would know what we want.

Do you speak with more consideration to your client, your friend, your boss, or your mate? We often don't give the same care, appreciation, and consideration to our mate as we do to others. We simply take our partner for granted. Often, we feel we are taken for granted, but if you are not getting enough respect, love, or appreciation from your partner, chances are you are not giving enough. If you don't like what you are receiving, examine what you are giving.

Relationships also change over time by either evolving or deterio-rating. This is not good or bad, it is just the way it is. The alternative would be stagnation, which is impossible at the Greater Self level. Although we like to fantasize that our relationships will last forever, the truth is that they eventually come to an end or change form, either by the death of one partner or other causes of separation. We must accept that endings are simply part of the cycle of change and are not, in and of themselves, negative. Everything changes. Pain takes center stage due to our resistance to change. The form of a relationship might change, but whether the person is in or out of our life, we will have a relationship with that person forever. If we are addicted to the form of the relationship, we will experience pain from change until we give up our addiction. Most of us are not addicted to the person but to the form.

WHAT WILL THEY THINK?

It is difficult enough for us to admit to ourselves that we have made an error in judgment but, what is even more difficult is to admit it to others. The possibility of hearing those dreaded words, "I told you so," is usually more than we are ready to face. Our concern for what others will think or say keeps us on the downward spiral of impossibil-ity. We may persist against our own better judgment simply to avoid being called a quitter or a loser, but being called a quitter or a loser by others is something we cannot deal with easily. In fact, one of our primary goals is to look good to others, so we concentrate on present-ing an image to the world rather than working on the true substance of who we are.

The bottom line is that *it does not matter what others think unless you think it matters.* Only you can make it important.

There is a story about Buddha. On his travels, he met a man who did not like him. The man kept insulting him in every possible way. This went on for many days and many miles.

Finally one day Buddha turned to the man and said, "May I ask you a question?"

"What?" the man replied.

"If someone offers you a gift and you decline to accept it, to whom does it then belong?"

The man said, "It belongs to the person who offered it."

Buddha smiled, "That is correct, so if I decline to accept your abuse, does it still not belong to you?"

The man was speechless and walked away.

The point is that, given the assumption that we operate from a solid spiritual base, it does not matter what others think about us or our actions.

When we are concerned about what others will think or say, we lose control over our performance process. Pressure is largely a response to the importance we place on something. Because it is important to do well, we pay more attention to what we are doing. The problem is that instead of paying attention to what we want to accomplish, and how we are going to do something we focus our attention on what others will think. This causes us to become more self-conscious. Anything that increases our self-consciousness will increase our chances of failing or choking under pressure, whether in sports, business, or emotional expression. The problem is that we become externally directed instead of internally directed.

Other people's opinions are just that. They are disguised as advice, but they are really nothing more than opinions. Whenever someone starts to tell you how you made a previous mistake, especially in their terms of failure, give them a strong response, letting them know that you do not *care* to hear their negative criticism. This is a time to clearly let it be known that they are not welcome to give you their opinion, especially when you did not invite them to do so. Make sure you don't give people invitations to make conclusions for you.

IS ONE PERSON EVER MORE AT FAULT IN AN ARGUMENT?

We'll always wonder if there was something more we could do when things go wrong, but in the end, it takes two people that are willing to give and take a little during uncomfortable discussions. There will always be a better way to say something to someone, but when one party cannot let go and forgive any misunderstandings, that person may not be worthy of your friendship, especially if you have been fair in your own admissions to them.

Being accepting and giving someone the benefit of the doubt is the only factor that matters in all the issues of misunderstanding. It takes two people who are willing to be a bit forgiving, understanding, and accepting. It is the one (or sometimes it may be both) who gives no chance to the other that makes the relationship an impossible one. If just one person cannot admit anything or say I'm sorry, then it is impossible to have a trusting relationship with that person. It's time to move on.

I have said it takes two willing people to resolve misunderstandings or make amends, but I've heard too long the idea that whenever there is conflict, it is always to be treated as an equal responsibility. If one party has done something that most people would consider egregious, let's say it is some kind of physical cruelty, the party who is the physical abuser is not going to stop if this belief system of equal responsibility is in place. The true offender never takes total responsibility for physically pounding on others. Instead, that person will keep diverting the issue by saying it is the other party's fault, too. The relationship cannot continue if the physical abuser is not going to take complete responsibility for actions that have no excuse. When you get to hitting, there is no excuse. I don't buy into letting criminal offenders off for their crimes of violence because their mother made them do it.

Conflicts in relationships can be resolved when a party who is doing socially and psychologically inappropriate things to another is willing to admit to the problem and do whatever it takes to eliminate this behavior. This does not necessarily mean that the other party is always completely innocent. It might be, but the other person also could be contributing to the incidents of abuse by doing things, either deliberately or unconsciously, that incite the abuser. The victim is totally responsible for having these experiences, because he or she could learn skills to defuse these battles or get out of the relationship. Even so, the victim is not responsible for the actual physical harm that occurred.

METAMESSAGES—WHAT WE REALLY MEAN WHEN WE SPEAK

Sometimes we want to pull away from relationships when we have had a misunderstanding. That's just the point. Many of the relationships we scrap might have worked out if we had the opportunity to really go heart-to-heart with a person about what lingers behind our conflicts. Often we are misunderstood or we misunderstand what certain communications really mean.

We read people differently based on our belief system combined with our perception of what others say and do. The tendency for us to have preconceived ideas about what communications mean is based on our life experiences. Our comprehension of what is communicated to us is filtered through our own linguistic understanding that was developed through childhood within our families, by friends, and on through our workplace and society.

Our cultural differences and our ways of storytelling and giving analogies can make us perceive words dramatically differently. On top of that, body language, facial expressions, and voice tones affect meaning as well.

We conceptualize what we think someone is saying through this filtering process and we each have a very different take on what someone has said to us. We can think someone that we just met is wonderful until he or she surprises us with a remark that seems rude; but to someone else, the person could be perceived as being friendly. Deborah Tannen, Ph.D., who wrote *That's NOT What I Meant!* terms this conceptualizing as *metamessages.*

Dr. Tannen gives an example of a Greek father whose daughter was expected to ask for permission if she wanted to go to a dance. Because he did not want to seem tyrannical, he never said no. But she could tell from the way he said yes whether or not he meant it. If he said something like, "Yes, of course, go," then she knew he thought it was a good idea. If he said something like, "If you want, you can go," then she understood that he didn't think it was a good idea, and she wouldn't go. His tone of voice, facial expression, and all the elements of conversational style gave her clues as to how he felt about her going.

This was an understood family style of interacting, where the father did not want to appear tyrannical, so he would be *indirect* in his communications. When his daughter would later marry, she could possibly have misunderstandings with her husband about what he meant when he would respond to her requests and suggestions.

There are a multitude of ways people give *metamessages* when they converse, and learning more about this could make a significant difference in making what seems to be impossible relationships become possible. *Metamessages* can be communicated by indirectness, joking (using irony, sarcasm, and figures of speech), being too direct with our honesty, linguistic signals, voice intonation, questioning (that may seem like interrogation), styles of complaining, manipulation, and persuasion.

IMPOSSIBLE EXPECTATIONS

In addition to *metamessages,* we also have ingrained ideas about what we *expect* of others that can cause further misunderstanding. There are two kinds of expectations. In the first instance, we expect others to *automatically perform politely* in a manner that we believe is appropriate or the right thing to do.

The other kind of expectation regards *accomplished performance.* This is the kind of attitude that leaders are so good at building up in others. They are able to motivate people to believe in something that they did not believe before and then help them to bring that expected vision into reality. Most people have to see it before they believe it. A leader can get others to believe it before they see it. This is the key to making the impossible possible.

However, if you get caught in someone else's expectancy trap, get out of there. The object is not for them to like you, the object is for them to listen to you. If they won't, then go. Nobody knows what you want except you. And nobody will care if you don't get it.

In order to change our own level of expectancy, we must have a strong belief in ourselves and our goals, but that does not mean we should expect everyone else to see things exactly the way we do. We *want* the differences in others to come forward in order to contribute to our goals, but as soon as we make harsh demands on others regarding their performance, we'll lose them quickly.

When it comes to expecting others to respond and perform as we anticipate, our level of expectancy is based on our perception or the *frame* from which we express ourselves. We can turn people off to us by what seems to be a small infraction of someone else's beliefs or by doing what seems morally unforgivable. Either way, complete opposition can happen in a moment.

FORGIVENESS

Relationships can be suddenly ended by one party who has kept count of numerous supposed infractions and suddenly makes a surprise blow by terminating the relationship. When others harm us verbally or physically or just hurt our feelings, they are often viewed by us as unforgivable. Life brings us all kinds of personal hurts, from broken promises and white lies to physical slaps and spankings. Most are forgivable, some are more difficult to forgive, but not everyone is willing to forgive others or themselves. The problem is that if we don't forgive, we carry around the excess negative baggage for the rest of our lives. This excess baggage contributes to the spiral of impossibility. Our resentment becomes part of our belief system, and we use it to justify either doing or not doing something. In many cases, it turns people into professional victims. As we learned earlier, if you perceive yourself as a victim, you also become a volunteer. You volunteer to stay where you are. The only way out is to forgive and let go.

Forgiveness is purely a selfish act. You are not doing it for them, you are doing it for yourself. This doesn't mean you have to like the person. You don't even have to associate with the person or contact him or her, but you must emotionally and sometimes physically release them. Don't let the memories drag you down into the spiral of impossibility. Realize that the payoff for not forgiving is too high. Not forgiving only makes you right. The question is, would you rather be right or would you rather be happy?

COMMUNICATION STYLE CAN
MAKE THE IMPOSSIBLE POSSIBLE

By not understanding personality differences and the resulting differences in communication style, we will eventually alienate ourselves, since all we can conclude is that others are *wrong,* and we are always right. Understanding people's belief systems, perceptions, and metamessages can make all the difference in having possible rather than impossible relationships.

Have you ever noticed that soap operas are dependent upon a blatant lack of communication in order to exist? The wife doesn't tell her husband she is pregnant, the sister doesn't tell the brother that they have a different father, the friend doesn't tell a friend that his business partner is embezzling. What we don't realize is that, in a sense, we are all miscommunicating almost as badly every day because we each have different perspectives on what certain phrases and statements mean.

Cultural differences and our family's communication style play a paramount role in our comprehension of what someone means when they speak. Lately, there is more public and professional discussion than ever about the differences in communication styles between men and women. The specific definitions and applications of male and female differences could make a book of its own, so I will refrain from detailing this as much as I would like.

By nature and necessity of brain function, we are constantly interpreting and conceptualizing what we hear people say. We can perceive whether people are joking or serious, mean or kind, rude or polite; or we can wonder whether a statement was directed at us or to someone else.

The problem is, how often do we ask for clarification *before* we end up feeling bothered by what someone says or does? More importantly, the real question is, do we give people the benefit of the doubt? We regularly give people the benefit of the doubt when they suddenly interrupt us, especially because the interrupter will usually show good reason by the subject of the interruption.

Why don't we give more of the benefit of the doubt to others more often in other kinds of situations? Usually it is because we reacted first. Then, why don't we resolve misunderstandings by being more willing to relinquish and give the benefit of the doubt in an effort to resolve misunderstandings? Usually we're too upset by then. We're sure the other person could only have meant the worst.

There are several ways to get clarification in order to prevent misunderstanding or to repair the damage from misunderstandings that already occurred. We can ask the other person to restate what he or she said in a new way so that we can be sure we understand the intention and meaning. We can also ask the other person if we are understanding the message correctly and rephrase the statement. By rephrasing the statement, we are *naming* the perception we believe we are hearing, thus gaining clarification.

Writing often elevates people to communicating from their Greater Self, as more care is given to each written word. The one thing that is lacking in writing, though, is tone of voice and all that the voice can imply. Although lack of voice intonation is a reason writing can often be misunderstood, the slowness of it and the fact that it is in print does make us take greater care in our choice of words. Additionally, re-reading what we wrote gives us the chance to notice whether our meaning is clear or whether there could be a double meaning in what we wrote.

GETTING OUT OF SOMEONE ELSE'S FRAME OF PERCEPTION

When we get into conflict, it is a result of our buying into someone else's perception rather than defusing a conflicting perception. As soon as someone says something we find offensive, we tend to jump in with our defense, causing a tumble.

There have been times when I forgot this when I wished I had just asked what else might be the matter and waited for a response, since upset people are often not really upset at us at all. They just seem to take it out on us because they couldn't help bursting out when we put one more stick on the camel's back (in their mind, at least). In other words, people who blow up at us might be misreading something we have said or done, but because they were already seriously stressed by other matters, they lost it when we were around. Of course, we forget to check, so we overreact to what they said. Since what they said to us is not really what is bothering them, any response in defense to their remark is not needed at all. Unfortunately, most of us are running around in survival mode, ready to defend and protect ourselves at a moment's notice.

NOT LISTENING CAN BE A DRASTIC MISTAKE

We can never stop learning when it comes to communication skills, which include verbal, written, and—what is *drastically* forgotten—our ability to listen. Specialists have been telling us for years that we only retain 10 percent of what we hear. If you think about it, in an all-day seminar, without taking notes, and especially without seeing visual aids, our retention is zilch.

Another way to look at the act of listening is, 10 percent of what we hear comes from words, 40 percent of what we hear comes from voice intonation, and 50 percent gets bungled up by our personal interpretation or is entirely lost by our lack of attention.

Now we're getting to the part about how much we *really* pay attention to what we hear others say. Our attention is usually focused on what we want to say next, while we hope the other person will soon finish. I catch myself doing this, and a business partner I was working with caught me at it, too.

My friend Gary suggested that I press my finger down while I talk, reminding myself to limit how much I say and stop so another can speak. Actually, I found that I need to do the reverse of what he suggested. Gary was right about my burning desire to jump in when someone else is speaking, so I have chosen to press my finger on the table or the arm of a chair while the other person is speaking in order to prevent my breaking in and to emphasize the importance of my listening.

What is a little amusing to me is that I think Gary *does* need to hold his finger down *while he talks* because my perception is that he gets too long-winded while he is speaking. So, whichever you are, long winded or an interrupter or, God forbid, both, press your finger down while you do what you ought to limit yourself from doing. It works.

HONESTY

Give people a little money and they'll lie, even on the witness stand. Where on earth do people get the idea that it's OK to lie? It's become an accepted public norm. Try never telling a lie—not even white lies. You don't have to tell white lies, you can find a way to diplomatically tell the truth. The only thing I try to avoid is telling people I don't want to see them at all. This is when the truth is truly painful to the other party. I will tell people that I don't seem to have the same interests as them, or that we don't have that much in common . . . in a careful way. It works with good communication skills. Usually, if I don't like getting together with someone, it's because he or she will not stop doing something I have asked that person not to do, so the person knows that is why I do not want to get together. I usually don't have to tell someone something that is critical or very rejecting.

Once you get into always telling the truth, it is amazing to notice what goes on within your mind and how you more clearly and more honestly perceive things. Being totally honest seems to focus our minds on being completely on purpose. When I am focused on a purpose, I have easy ways to communicate honestly without causing anyone pain. When your life is on purpose, you will find it easy to be honest.

GOOD INFLUENCE OR BAD INFLUENCE?

How do we know who is a good influence on us and who is not? How do we know if we are having an intuitive, accurate hunch about someone and not a rush to judgment based on our own previous experiences? Perhaps a person we have just met is demonstrating only one facet of his or her personality, when there is much more to get to know. We all have our fleeting moments of temporary annoyance, but often we decide that what we have seen in someone we have just met is solidly who they are.

By using our intuition and having a clear understanding of ourselves as we relate to others, we can continually enhance our ability to know who is good for us to be around.

When we get to the possibility of longer-term and deeper relationships, whether it be business or a love partner, choosing who to partner up with is a gamble. We take a gamble and accept the risk of being hurt, rejected, and disappointed. Investing in a partnership is going beyond risking the possibility of failed expectations or rejection when our partner falls short of the perfection we perceived at first. As we choose to deepen our relationship with another, we must look at the complementary opposite side of love.

The issue is to free ourselves from the imaginary chains that bind us. The chains are people, or how we perceive people to have a hold on us. Do we want to keep choosing the same kinds of people over and over again in our lives, so we can keep learning the same lessons over and over again? Maybe our biggest challenge with some individuals is simply to realize how we handle them rather than the issue we think we have going on with them.

The misuse of loyalty can enslave us to people, institutions, and things. Take a look at the organizations you are involved with. Will you allow yourself to be enslaved by an organization's extremes in competitiveness? How far should we go in competitiveness as opposed to cooperation? Consider what competition did regarding the bashing of Nancy Kerrigan's knee before the 1994 Winter Olympics.

You may be victimized by the very organizations or associations you endorse if you get caught up in their intense levels of competition. Take another look at competition and ask yourself if you are not being victimized by the system within which you work. An organization is out of control if it takes competitiveness to an extreme where people feel threatened.

How you use your loyalty is totally up to you. Being loyal to your own plans and loyal to things that support your purpose and goals is fine, but an executive who can't leave his desk doesn't belong behind the desk at all. It is your choice to chain yourself to stress, worry, tension, and burdens or to be fulfilled by your devotion to things that satisfy your health, happiness, and success.

SELF-LOVE VS. LOVING OTHERS

The '80s has been coined the "me" decade. The emphasis of most self-help books and seminars was on serving our own needs first in order to better enable us to serve others. In the '90s, there seems to be a backlash against putting self-love before others. Many are quick to blame society's troubles on the me generation. The generalization is that, instead of caring about others, the me-first advocates were more interested in serving themselves.

Perhaps you feel this way. Admittedly, self-love is not the cure for all of society's ills; however, it is the basis of sound mental health. On the surface, it may appear noble to love and serve others first. In all honesty though, we cannot ignore our own needs at the expense of putting others first. It simply does not make sense. You can't give something you don't already have. If you want to borrow five dollars from me, I must first have the five dollars, no matter how much I want to help you. If I give you the five dollars and I need it, eventually I will resent you. If I have taken care of my own needs first, I will be emotionally, psychologically, physically, and spiritually solvent. Instead of trying to give from lack, I can give from abundance. When I give from abundance, I am giving from surplus, so there is an ample supply left over for me. As a result, both of us are stronger as individuals and as partners in the relationship.

Much has been written about the power of love. Love is two people celebrating the fact that they are one. It goes beyond you are and I am. Real love goes beyond just two people. It is a mutual bond that is greater than the individuals and keeps the two greater than the one.

Without love of self and others, we are impotent to change. A loveless life will be barren and always seem impossible. Love is the most powerful force we have for personal success. As a working definition of love, we shall call it any action we take for the physical, mental, or spiritual enhancement of ourselves or others. Love is the action that strengthens our self-esteem and self-worth by helping ourselves and others to see strengths instead of weaknesses. Love creates a focus on our assets instead of our liabilities. Self-love motivates us to care for ourselves physically and mentally by investing effort in physical fitness, a healthy diet, sexual satisfaction, expanding the mind, and experiencing joyful days.

Sometimes it is not easy to love ourselves or others. Anyone I have ever met who did not love themselves or others based their love on some action or lack of appropriate action that did not meet their expectations. This occurs because we are judging our worthiness or the worthiness of others by actions. The key is to love who you are rather than what you do or have. Remember, what you do or have is temporary. Who you are has and will be with you for eternity. By separating actions from the person, the actor from the performance, we can still love the person but not love the action. This is the true meaning of unconditional love and the foundation of all possibility relationships.

ELIMINATE THE NEGATIVE, ATTRACT THE POSITIVE

In order to fully experience our possibilities, we must get away from people who are constantly sad, pessimistic, grouchy, or negative in general. Do not join them in their misery. Remember, give them the benefit of the doubt by first telling them that you would prefer to keep things on a more upbeat scale, but if they don't change their way of interacting with you, you must either disassociate yourself from them completely or change the form of the relationship from closeness to casual and infrequent interaction.

We want can-do people around us who see all the reasons and possibilities in how things *can* be done. If you were to hire a consultant, would you select and pay someone to tell you what you cannot do? You want an advisor who can enhance your perception of the possibilities at hand. We must surround ourselves with people with high self-esteem, people who can tell us how to get the job done, how to make it happen for us.

While we're busy recognizing the characteristics of the kind of people that can influence our win factor, we must consider that *we* must have those same characteristics and abilities. Winners know how to separate facts from the opinions of others, and although they may lose a few battles now and then, they never take on the role of being helpless victims.

Winners have a sense of timing and value their time, using it to their advantage. They may enjoy life as much as anyone else, but they don't seek gratification during a time that is essential for accomplishments.

Winners know that their personal attitude plays a major role in their success as they set themselves up to succeed. Winners live in a state of *positive expectancy.* Since they expect to win, they do. Winners have this faith in themselves as they know that they are working in alignment with something much greater than themselves. They realize that they use their intuition and faith to know when the time is right to take certain actions or steps toward their goals.

When we have the character of a winner, we accept winning as a natural and inevitable state of events. Choose yourself first as a winning personality who chooses and is chosen by other winners to have a powerful influence on their life.

FIFTEEN KEYS TO GREAT POSSIBILITY RELATIONSHIPS

1. *Be true to yourself.* Don't give your power away. The only true authority figure is within yourself. Good leaders are scarce, so follow yourself.

2. *Shed the need for approval or recognition.* Emotions leading us by the horns can tie us into *im*possible relationships.

3. *Continually learn more and more interpersonal skills.* Read books, go to seminars, learn from your experiences with others, and learn from others' experiences. You get treated in life the way you *train* people to treat you, but first you've got to train yourself.

4. *Select possibility seekers.* Notice the way people talk. If they talk about problems, do they discuss them with possibilities in mind? If not, suggest that they do, and you'll be glad to help.

5. *Do your best to enhance your relationships.* Keep doing your best, with learned skills, to either mend or enhance relationships; otherwise, go in a new direction.

6. *Keep your own thoughts free of* **impossibility thinking.** Don't be judgmental, blaming, and otherwise be *im*possible yourself. No one does it to you. You do it to *yourself, through* other people.

7. *Accept differences.* Many of our relationships might have been worked out, rather than left behind. When two or more possibility thinkers get together, all kinds of misunderstandings can be worked through. Remember, we all have different *frames* of mind that we are communicating and relating from.

8. *Don't set yourself up or set up others with* **impossible expectations.** No one else will ever be able to give you exactly what you want. When the going gets tough, nearly everyone leaves.

9. *Watch who influences you, and how.* Always check to see how much you are letting your relationships influence you, and in which way.

10. ***Look for common-goal and team relationships.*** People with the same goals and especially the same purpose are ten times more productive.

11. ***Find mentors and model what you admire about them.*** Learn from your mentors, but remember that you are the only one to make your choices and decisions in the long run.

12. ***Honest possibility seekers are a requirement.*** Picture this: a seemingly positive possibility seeker who is dishonest. This spells trouble. These characteristics indicate a person who is a manipulator or even a con artist. With this person's charm and enthusiasm, he or she could sell you a bill of goods. Honest possibility thinkers are able and willing to work through anything with you in creating the possibilities *you* intend.

13. ***Believe that you deserve success and happiness.*** Visualize yourself having what you desire and preplay yourself taking action and doing the activities that lead you to the successful completion of your goals.

14. ***Expand your circle of possibility.*** Use your creative perception, which includes dynamic of boldness, not hesitation, worry, or fear.

15. ***Use the impossible to make possibilities.*** Use adversity as a force that propels you. Shift the initial emotions you may feel (burdened, controlled, anxiety, etc.) to the dynamic energy boosting emotions of hope, courage, engagement, power, and so on.

CHAPTER 10

Possible Choices

The Greater Self with a Greater Plan of Action

It is one thing to know that we can make the impossible possible, but what is more important is doing something about it. Hopefully, the chapters in this book have motivated and inspired you to take action. If not, perhaps this chapter will.

At the risk of appearing senile, I have taken the liberty of repeating some of the important points you have already read. My goal is to inspire you to release the power of your Greater Self with a greater plan of action.

Clear thinking and an empowered sense of self is the necessary foundation from which to turn the impossible into the possible. When we plan our lives and set goals with the powerful meaning of purpose, we will remain on track regardless of any obstacles in our path. The more *clear* we are about what we want, the more *power* we will have in achieving our goals.

MAKING CHOICES

The only thing in life we have no choice about is *making* choices. Everything we experience is the result of our conscious or unconscious choices. How much are we aware of the importance of every single choice we make? Are we aware how far any tiny decision that we make may take us?

In some way, either through conscious or unconscious choices, we *set ourselves up* for everything that comes into our life, good or bad, happy or sad, success or failure. This includes all facets of our life, be it business, relationships, health, or personal affairs. In addition, every choice has a natural result leading to further choices of a similar nature.

Before we can free ourselves from impossible situations, we must take responsibility for our own choices. There is no room in our minds or time in our lives to blame everyone or everything else. All this does is fill our hearts and minds with negative emotions like resentment, which blocks our ability to see new possibilities. Our attitude of victimization can leave us barricaded in our own prison of *im*possibility. Instead, it is our choice to change our attitude to one filled with unlimited possibilities by taking responsibility for where we are and where we want to be.

Our conscious awareness, through possibility choices, is our way of changing impossible situations into possible opportunities. Our goal in life should be to convert every experience, through the dominant thought of possibility thinking, into temporary challenges on our path to becoming our Greater Self. It is not enough to *see* the possibility, we must *become* the possibility.

We have already learned that there is no way to avoid problems. The real secret is the way we choose to *respond* to problems and life situations. Put simply, it is not *what* happens to us that controls our present and future, but what we *think* and *believe* about the events in our lives. This means that we must be willing to accept what has happened, to accept where we are right now, and to take responsibility for changing our present situation. We could view it this way:

What is, *was.*

What was, *is.*

My past will always be *the way it was.* I can't change that.

What will be, is up to me.

I must give up my interpretation of the way it is to have it **the way I want it.**

Once we realize that this *is* reality and that things are the way they are, we can change our thoughts and therefore change our experience.

As Shakespeare so astutely observed, life is our stage and we are all actors. We tend to act out the scripts we have been told to play. One way or the other, our life is a continuous series of scenes in the play. We can write a new script at any time. All it takes is a conscious choice to envision our life script with new possibilities.

POSITIVE LESSONS

We must remember not *to personalize* everything that we think happens to us. The problem with personalizing every experience is that it not only influences the way things were and the way things are, but the way things *will be* in the future. What has happened to us is only part of a positive lesson, and positive lessons are not always perceived to be taught in positive ways.

Whether we like it or not, life *is* fair. Life's little traumas give us opportunities to make better choices, to stretch us beyond where we have been before, and to expand our circle of possibility. Unfortunately, most people would rather stay stuck where they are than change their impossible situations. In fact, most people would rather be *certain* they're miserable, than *risk* being happy. They keep doing whatever they have been doing that hasn't worked because they're afraid to risk. All the while, they never realize that the greatest risk of all is not risking. If we don't risk, we can be sure nothing will change.

Turning the surprise of pain or disappointment into positive lessons is essential to personal growth. If life didn't push us sometimes, there would be very little change for the better. There must be stimulation to trigger new thought or change for the better. This creates discontent with the way things are or the way we want things to be. Without discontent, there is no motivation or stimulation to change.

PERCEPTION ADJUSTMENT—SEE
PROBLEMS AS ONLY TEMPORARY

We must see problems as *temporary* and look for the complementary opposite in all that happens to us. We must look for possibilities as we *learn from adversity,* and use the spark of personal challenge to propel us forward. Robert Leighton said it this way: "Learn from adversity! Adversity is the diamond dust heaven polishes its jewels with!"

We should practice awareness modification. This requires changing our beliefs by learning from adversity. The problem is that the more investment we have in our beliefs, the harder it is to change them. Defending our beliefs and trying to prove ourselves right only serves to waste our valuable time and resources and delays our ability to change our situation.

A possibility thinker is always willing to change and knows he or she is always *part of the answer.* A possibility thinker sees an *answer* in every problem. Unfortunately, the *im*possibility thinker just sees the problem and thinks he or she is the effect instead of the cause.

It's our choice. We will always find whatever we are looking for. We have a choice to turn the situation around and to find the complementary opposite and make our own reality. If we are caught up in taking everything that happens to us personally and defending our beliefs and actions, we will be so busy protecting our false sense of autonomy that the solution will be out of our reach. We cannot find the solution if we keep looking at the problem. When we focus on the solution, it will be revealed to us, because whatever we are ready for is ready for us. All we have to do is look for it.

ENDINGS MAKE GREATER BEGINNINGS

We must learn from our experiences, forget our past track record, and take each moment as a new beginning. Otherwise, we will keep repeating the same old thing. If we argue long enough for our limitations, they're ours. It goes like this:

> If you keep *doing*
> what you have been *doing,*
> you will keep *getting*
> what you have been *getting.*

The rewards in life go to those who are willing to give up the past. Experience is the best teacher, provided we become the best students. When something doesn't work out the way we expected, we need to leave the experience behind us, but take with us the message or indicator that guides us to a new beginning. There is no time to waste with denial, resistance, avoidance, and criticism or blame. Our habit is to make the same old choices and have the same old reactions. Let the experience end and make a new beginning through each stage of any

process of work or challenge. Welcome all of life's challenges as perfect messages guiding us to shift our course.

CHAOS BRINGS NEW ORDER AND
NEW POSSIBILITIES

When life seems to shake things up through ever-changing circumstances, we must use times of disorder or chaos to see the variety of
possibilities that come our way. Even though times of disruption and
change may seem like chaos, these times are actually *perfect timing* as
new possibilities will always come before us. Chaos stirs up our perception, allowing us to refocus and redirect our actions. We have the
choice to perceive change as a time of chaos and *im*possibility, or as
perfect timing for new possibilities to appear.

If we view chaos as *im*possibility, we will kick into our survival
mode and close our doors to possibilities. On the other hand, a falsely
positive attitude can mean putting our head in the sand and avoiding
problems. We must face problems head on, with a new attitude of
seeing the possibilities. If we put our head in the sand, we block our
sense of self—our Greater Self—where the possibilities and solutions
lie. Our Greater Self is personally empowered and can better realize
and assess possibilities. Finding winning possibilities requires shifting
our emphasis from *won't* power to *will*power. Remember, It doesn't
matter what you *can* do, what really matters is what you *will* do.

RISKS AND REWARDS

If we don't take risks, we can't take quantum leaps that can propel
us forward more rapidly. Our *rewards* in life will always be in direct
proportion to the *risks* we are willing to take. Great inventors try
thousands of times until they reach a discovery. Taking risks should be
as much a part of our lives and as easily understood as the everyday
mistake.

Probably the strongest reason why we don't make certain choices is
our fear of mistakes or things not working out as we expected. Worst
of all, others might think we made a mistake. Mistakes are an everyday part of life. In fact, I tell people if you are not making at least ten
mistakes every day, something is wrong. You are not moving forward.

This attitude is currently accepted in many corporations that are beginning to encourage their employees to take risks. Corporations think risk taking is worth it. A current trend in corporate training programs includes the recommendation that corporations welcome their employees to take risks and positively reward them for doing so, even if certain actions and plans might not work out. They are advised to look for what did work and what was a good idea and then improve on the original idea. Certainly, if corporations are willing to invest in risk taking, the reason is that in the end there is a higher return when the innovative ideas of their people finally pay off.

POSSIBILITIES IN ACTION

Getting on Purpose

Our purpose makes our goals believable because we are connected to the greatest personal benefits that fulfill us. *Why* we do something is more important than *how* we do it. When we have purpose, we will always find the path of least resistance guiding us with possibilities toward our goal.

The positive focus of purpose keeps us from being distracted and can also prevent our becoming too emotional when problems arise because our eyes and mind are focused on something we truly desire. If we get caught up in the small, day-to-day busy stuff, we could miss our chance to give the commitment needed to achieve the greater things in life. People who fail to achieve their real desires in life do so because they *major* in *minor* things.

Goals and Planning

Planning is the creative process put into action, and goals set mileposts of accomplishment with specific measurements of results and time frames. Goals set our strategy into action and ensure our commitment. They motivate in two ways: first by *seeing the measurable results* produced, and then by giving us *checkpoints* to ensure that we maintain our *momentum*.

The goals we choose must be something we are willing to work for on a daily basis. Otherwise, they are not the right investment for our contribution of time, resources, and energy. When our goals are set with clarity of purpose, then planning, scheduling, and related prioritizing is a breeze. Necessary adjustments are just part of the ongoing process in getting what we want.

MANAGE YOUR TIME, YOUR
ENERGY, AND YOUR MIND

Planning and scheduling how and when we *intend* to create what we want is paramount in these fast-paced times. We don't have to get anxious about our time, otherwise we'll make rash decisions and have an ineffective approach toward getting what we want. Our time is vitally important, but it must be managed with clarity and peace of mind. With purpose, our passion kicks in gear, giving us the creative energy we want and need to make work a true pleasure. We always find time to do what we love.

In most people's minds, work is doing something we don't want to do to earn money as compensation, but if we are truly suited for the work we do, we will love doing it and enjoy the compensation. Being suited has to do with two things: our purpose and our instinctive talent, which usually matches our purpose. The key is discovering and focusing on things we love to do. These are our natural talents. The only way to succeed in the long run is to get very good at what we love to do, because we can never get good enough at something we are not suited for. True happiness is loving what you do and getting someone else to pay you to do it.

Having the overview of purpose and the accompanying values gives us the big picture we need to see ourselves reaching our goals. With this overview, our planning and scheduling come more easily and effectively, like the path of least resistance. If we do not value our time, energy, and resources as precious, we can deplete them by allowing *im*possible distractions to take us away from what we want most. With our Greater Self intact and aligned with our true purpose, we know exactly when to do exactly what we need to do with greater effectiveness.

FOCUSING OUR TIME AND ENERGY

Our energy is our most important resource, and therefore it must be protected from *im*possibility deterrents and directed in a progressive focus toward the possibilities we select. Here are the ways we can simplify our lives to allow for possibilities to come to us easily.

Focus on Simplifying Your Life

Figuratively and *literally,* clean all your closets. Get rid of all the debris and dirty laundry. Make *room* for new possibilities.

Organize and Prioritize Your Life

Assess how much time you spend in various areas of your life such as social, spouse/love partner, family, exercise, alone, work, vocation, hobbies and club activities, and relaxing, and then balance them out more evenly.

Mental/Psychological Management

Frequently do a mental checkup regarding your perspectives on your experiences. Seek areas for self-improvement of your interpersonal management.

> Never grow tired of growing!—
> When your mind is tired, exercise your body.
> When your body is tired, exercise your mind.
> —Anonymous

FAILING BY NOT DOING

Impossibility thinkers are usually passive. They let things happen to them instead of directing their lives and determining their outcome. They are usually afraid of change in any form, even if there is no risk involved. New situations frighten them or make them anxious. They are unwilling to answer the door when opportunity knocks.

Our success is measured by our ability to complete things, and yet whatever we have not accomplished is what we have *chosen* to keep from ourselves. *Im*possibility thinkers who believe things can't be done will go out and prove they are *right*.

Procrastination is directly related to our *im*possibility thinking and emotions. With impossibility thinking, we can dread doing tasks that appear to be drudgery when it is only our attitude that makes us perceive this. An old southern grandmother always said, "Thinkin' on it is worse than doin' on it."

The typical excuse for procrastination is to say we don't know what to do or how to do something. An *im*possibility thinker says, "I don't know." A possibility thinker says, "Let's find out."

It has also been said, "It is better to have tried and failed, than to have failed to try." I believe the *only* failure is not to have tried at all, but that *every* effort we take, no matter what the results, is a success for having taken action.

We've heard the phrase, "Good things come to those who wait." This may be true when we are motivated and we have already given it all we've got, but for those who just wait, I would say, "Things that come to those who wait may be the things left by those who got there first." We must take action, otherwise we will be left behind by those who were willing to take a risk and take action. Our life will be about trying to catch up. Even though risks are involved, you will find that it is much easier to *keep* up than to *catch up*. When we have an opportunity and don't take it, we've already made our choice. Not to decide is to decide.

YOU MUST BE SICK AND TIRED OF BEING SICK AND TIRED

Our motivation to take action will occur when it becomes more difficult to suffer than to change; in other words, when we become sick and tired of being sick and tired. Our habits that bring us pain are more comfortable for us than the fear and discomfort we may feel about doing new things in a new way. Why is it so hard for us to let go of certain counterproductive actions and decisions when the signs are there telling us that we have made these mistakes before? Our survival mode is fooling us into thinking we are avoiding pain when we are actually about to create the same old thing all over again.

Usually, before most of us will take the new road, we have to be in more pain than our perceived fear of the new road. Everything we do comes from our need to *avoid* pain and our desire to *gain pleasure*. *Both* are biologically driven and constitute the *controlling force in our life*. The desire to avoid pain tends to be the greater motivator rather than seeing new possibilities as positive opportunities.

Thought plus **emotion** creates **conviction**. Your **conviction** creates *your* **reality**. It is our choice to use our emotions as an energy force that shows us self-defeating impossibilities, or we can shift these emotions into energy boosters as we view possibilities with enthusiasm, resilience, creative spirit, and a personal sense of empowered competence.

All of our emotions move us in some way. Emotion is energy in motion. What is important to understand is that not all emotions are limiting. We have both limiting emotions that are energy sappers and expanding emotions that are energy boosters. Your choice to see *im*possibilities or see possibilities is the lens you select in perceiving things with negative emotions or uplifting and motivating emotions. It is then your choice to limit or expand your circle of possibility.

YOU HAVE NOTHING TO LOSE UNTIL YOU GIVE UP

A possibility thinker says, "It may be difficult, but it's possible." An *im*possibility thinker says, "It may be possible, but it's too difficult."

Why do we give up? Is it because we've tried before and then perceived ourselves as having failed, therefore our planned desires become unfulfilled dreams rather than something possible and still achievable? Have some of our experiences seemed painful and therefore we fear reaching for the brass ring? Even the concept of the brass ring seems to imply the unattainable. That is *not* what the brass ring concept is about. The brass ring is right there. Others have grasped the brass ring and so can we. Certainly, most of the goals we set are ones others have achieved before. If this is so, then you can achieve them as well. A possibility thinker says, "I will!" and succeeds. An *im*possibility thinker says, "I'll try," and fails. If we have some setbacks, we must not give up. Each *no* brings us that much closer to a *yes.* When we persist at something with consistent intention, we can *break through* to the success we want.

If we perceive past losses as catastrophic and painful because we chose to react that way before, we will resort to habit and look to the past as the controlling factor for our future. By setting step-by-step goals where we can see results along the way, then, if we get a bit off the course we anticipated, we can adjust it without catastrophic losses.

EXPECT WHAT YOU WANT

If we are not moving toward what we want, we don't really want it. The best way to *predict* our future is to *create* it. If we don't believe it and live it, we must not think we are worthy of it. The end result is that we always attract what we feel worthy of.

You will either live up to or down to your *expectations* of yourself and your future. The truth of the matter is, in life, you don't get what you *want,* you get what you *expect.* Everyone *wants* health, wealth, and happiness, but they don't have it. The problem is they want it but they don't expect it. If we don't expect it, we will not create it and attract it. We must believe that we *deserve* what we most desire. The conflict comes from believing "I want this, but I only deserve that." Whatever we deserve is *really* whatever we choose to *expect* to happen.

We want to train our conscious and subconscious mind to consistently see possibilities, not *im*possibilities. The mind is a marvelous thing. If you will make the *decision,* your subconscious will make the *provision.* The conscious and subconscious can either assist us in creating the possible, or convince us that what we desire is *im*possible. The choices we make and the subsequent results we get are determined by how we use our conscious and subconscious mind.

The bottom line is that our thoughts create our reality. If we are focused on the negative, our subconscious will direct us to people, places, and circumstances to prove that we are right. In order to preserve sanity, the subconscious always seeks to prove that what we are thinking is in fact true. Our job is to present ideas to the subconscious that compel it to direct us to what we want instead of what we don't want—to the possible instead of the impossible.

CREATE A NEW HABIT OF
POSSIBILITY THINKING

Listen to your intuitive hunches and give them full consideration as you make choices. These are hunches like, "I have the feeling it's going to rain; better take my raincoat." What happens to you when you get hunches regarding important decisions? We must practice listening to our intuition more often so that when the larger-scale decisions come along, we can go within for the final answers. Our minds must be open and uncluttered to catch these important internal messages. The mind is like a parachute; it works best when it is open, not filled with worry or fear. Fear causes us to make rash decisions, and fear is the mind-talk that prevents you from hearing your intuition.

If we have purpose, which is an *inner* commitment, then where else but within can we find the best answers regarding the choices we make? If we think something outside of ourselves is the cause of our problem, we tend to look outside of ourselves for the answer. That's fine for collecting information, but then we must go within and check all that we know, including new possibilities, against our internal awareness for making a decision that has purpose, clarity, and overview. Instinctively, this is where our wisdom lies . . . within us.

Taking the time (most often it would only take a minute) to look for inner solutions is how we can make our smartest decisions, because we are giving our minds the chance to run the possibility by our fullest mental capacity, using both the right and left sides of our brains.

Most of us become so influenced by others that we can be lured with *their* ideas of what choices we should make, and then we are vulnerable to miscalculating the real value or viability of the options presented to us. We must get in the habit of putting on the brakes for a moment and going within, using our clearest mental capacities (right brain/left brain) to assess our own possibilities. When we get caught up in the short-term gain, usually found in the quick fix American personal management style, we do not consider the possible long-term pain that can result from hasty, externally influenced decisions. It is essential that our self-worth be stronger than the emotional sensation of rejecting the ideas of others.

IMAGINATION MAKES OUR
POSSIBILITIES LIMITLESS

There are several ways our imagination expands our circle of possibility. We go beyond reason and logic by adding the dynamic of creative thinking, which triggers our mind to present more possibilities to us from what we know. By using our imagination, we can think of new possibilities with the resources available to us; we perceive more. Our imagination expands our possibilities by showing us ways to interface or connect creative thinking and our imagination. Our open-mindedness makes us receptive to new possibilities coming to us like a magnet. We can solve problems with our imagination, which gives us room for expansion.

Imagination and brainstorming allow us to reconstruct or rework our information in order to create plans and goals that enable us to consider possibilities that were originally not in our mind. We can reconsider our options for accomplishing things and actually expand upon the envisioned end result.

For example, if you plan to build a boat, you can think of additional resources for materials, and then with creative thinking you realize that you can build a different, bigger, or better boat than you originally thought. The same imaginative expansion of possibilities can be applied to longer-term goals such as career planning.

Imagination solves problems by *creating possibilities* and anchoring our brain into *visualizing what we desire as possible.* When we envision ourselves having what we want, we preplay it in our minds as truly possible. To a great degree, you can control your own destiny. You are what is expandable.

INTENTION EXPANDS POSSIBILITIES

The key to success is to have dominant thought patterns that are totally aligned with what we want instead of what we don't want. This is our creative intention. If we are thinking about what we don't want, it becomes the dominant thought in our head that drives our brain's neurology. To the extent that we focus on what we don't want, we will create it. If we want money but focus on avoiding poverty, we will unconsciously create poverty. Our dominant thought will cause us to miss possibilities for what we want because we are looking for what we don't want.

Intention creates *attention* and expansion of possibilities that will come to us. We move toward what we picture in our mind and the intention drives us as an energy source. Wherever the mind goes, the energy flows. Whatever you give your energy to is what you will have more of. We don't get what we *want,* we get what we *expect.* When we preplay in our minds what we expect, our subconscious is compelled to find a way to make it possible.

FREE UP YOUR MIND FOR
CREATIVE GENIUS

Allow your creative genius to come to the forefront of your mind rather than bogging your mind down with the way things were in the past or with the possibility of failure. We need to use practical, day-to-day techniques to clear our heads for creativity, whether it is exercise, taking a break, or contemplation during a walk.

Practice staying in the moment. We tend to look at everything from some point of reference, and usually it's from some point in the past. If not the past, then it's what we imagine in the future regarding possible or *im*possible repercussions. We've got to perceive matters in the *now* with what we know *now*.

We can redirect our creative energy by consciously directing our thoughts as we concentrate on what we want to achieve. Here is a daily exercise you can do and it only takes a few minutes.

Mental Exercise to Focus and Direct Your Creative Mind

1. **Release** whatever is frustrating you. Often we think about or worry about things before we go to bed or when we wake up, so address them, clear them up, and get them out of your mind.

2. **State** to yourself that you are enacting certain improvements in your habits or character such as being more tolerant or controlling your temper. We will feel much better if we start the day with a clean slate. Remember the point about being in the *now*.

3. **Define what you want as a goal(s)**. Even if the goal or goals are for the long term, we must focus on actions to take today. They must be clearly defined, because if you don't, you might get something different from what you had in mind. Suppose you just say you want a lot of money. Your subconscious mind hasn't a clue what that means and therefore your mind cannot direct your thoughts toward specifics that will help you get what you want. Goals need to be measurable. If you want a certain amount of money, set a goal for a specific amount, but also, you can set a goal of a higher, ultimate amount, giving yourself a range. This way you can set a clearly achievable amount, and

yet when you set the higher amount, you expand your possibilities.

4. **Visualize** yourself *actively* having and enjoying what you wish. Sometimes I think our success almost entirely relies on setting visual images and affirming them by visualizing them as real.

Don't get so caught up in how busy you are that you skip starting your day with a clear vision of the results you want, because when you take a few minutes to do this exercise, you raise your chances of getting what you want substantially. Ultimately, this would be a daily routine, just as important as planning the things you will do for the day.

CHOOSE TO LIVE THE LIFE YOU WANT

*Im*possibility thinkers focus on *making a living*. Possibility thinkers focus on *making a life*.

When we work with the mind-set of just making a living, just getting by, we limit our possibilities. In an interview with Barbara Walters, Dustin Hoffman said his tombstone should read, "I knew this was going to happen!" That's funny, but it is a satirical remark on the perceived downside of life. We have a choice to either accept that life is predestined and that we cannot change things, or we can choose to live in a world of possibilities.

Shirley MacLaine made a choice to live her life differently, as she changed herself from being an *im*possibility thinker to a possibility thinker. In her autobiographical movie, *Out on a Limb*, she realized that her fears created her reality, making her resistant to anything that is new or different. If someone said something to her that was new, it was threatening to the point where she said she could not think straight.

This is how she worded her profound realization: "I always reacted negatively when I heard something that disturbed me or that I couldn't understand. . . . Did I *identify* myself by what I couldn't understand or by what frightened me . . . or, could *life actually be defined more by its possibilities* than by its limitations? And, was I on the threshold of understanding that there might be people out there that actually lived that way . . . with no sense of limitation?"

POSSIBILITY CREDO

There are many tools presented throughout this book that you can use to turn impossible situations into possible opportunities. Not all of them will apply to you. Mark and underline the ones that you feel will help you to understand yourself better and motivate you to change your life from this moment on.

In addition, I encourage you to read and memorize the following possibility credo. It sums up the essence of this book and will help direct your thinking to accepting the way things are, to be responsible for your choices, and to motivate you to use your resources to turn the impossible into the possible.

> I realize that life is fair, regardless of what happens.
>
> I accept things as the way they are before I can change.
>
> I know whenever I solve a problem, another problem will take its place.
>
> I understand that all problems are just possible opportunities in disguise.
>
> I focus on the solution, not the problem.
>
> I always assume my Greater Self knows a better way to do things.
>
> I either push, pull, or get out of the way, but I keep moving forward.
>
> I am willing to take risks and make mistakes.
>
> I am a person of action. If I say I'll do it, I do it.
>
> I keep my promises, especially those to myself.
>
> I never give up, because I know possibility thinkers never quit; *im*possibility thinkers never win.

Finally, please remember that as you make choices for turning the impossible into the possible through the greater plan of action for your Greater Self

You must *be*	(Who you are—your Greater Self)
before you can *do,*	(Change the impossible to the possible)
and you must *do*	(Take action)
before you can *have.*	(What you want—the possible)

BIBLIOGRAPHY

Ainsworth-Land, George T. *Grow or Die: The Unifying Principle of Transformation.* New York: Wiley, 1973. This reference was made near the Alvin Toffler reference.

Allenbaugh, Eric. *Wake-up Calls.* Austin, Tex.: Discovery Publications, 1992.

Borysenko, Joan. *Fire in the Soul: A New Psychology of Spiritual Optimism.* New York: Warner Books, 1993. Chapter 6: little deaths, dark nights of the soul.

Cameron, Julia. *The Artist's Way: A Spiritual Path to Higher Creativity.* Los Angeles, Ca: Jeremy P. Tarcher/Perigee, 1992. Chapters 5 and 7: Gateways list was inspired by her chapter titles, plus chapter 5, C. J. Jung's synchronicity quote, story about her in moviemaking.

Cramer, Kathryn D. *Staying on Top When Your World Turns Upside Down.* New York: Viking, 1990. The Emotional Rate Sheet was inspired by this book, but different words were used.

Flanigan, Beverly. *Forgiving the Unforgivable.* New York: Collier Books/Maxwell Macmillan, 1992. Chapter 9, the Process of Forgiveness.

Fritz, Robert. *The Path of Least Resistance.* Salem, Mass.: DMA, 1984. Early chapters and chapter 7: creative process, path of least resistance, getting what you want, law of nature that energy goes toward what you want.

Iacocca, Lee A., with William Novak. *Iacocca: An Autobiography.* New York: Bantam Books, 1984. Chapter 8 under subhead, Using Adversity as an Energy Booster.

MacLaine, Shirley. *Out on a Limb.* New York: Bantam Books, 1983. Chapter 10: Her statement was directly from her movie of the same title.

Peters, Thomas J. *In Search of Excellence: Lessons from America's Best-Run Companies.* New York: Harper & Row, 1982.

————*Thriving on Chaos: Handbook for a Management Revolution.* New York: Knopf, Distributed by Random House, 1987, 1988. Chapter 2, subhead The Asset of Persistence with Flexibility, specifically referred to both the Tom Peters book listed here and above.

Rohn, James E. *The Treasury of Quotes.* Tex.: Jim Rohn International, 1993. Rohn is quoted in several places in the book, where his name is mentioned.

Tannen, Deborah. *That's NOT What I Meant! How Conversational Style Makes or Breaks Your Relations with Others.* New York: Morrow, 1986. Chapter 9: metamessages, framing.

Toffler, Alvin. *The Third Wave.* New York: Morrow, 1980. Both Alvin Toffler books, listed here and below, were cited in text.